Penguin Books
Psmith in the City

P. G. Wodehouse was born in 1881, and educated
at Dulwich College. He was in the Hong Kong
and Shanghai Bank for two years and then got a
job on the 'By the Way' column of the old *Globe*.
His first stories were school stories written for
The Captain, in one of which Psmith made his first
appearance. He paid a visit to America in 1904,
and another in 1909 when he sold two short stories
for $300 apiece, and decided to remain there.
Eventually he sold a serial to the *Saturday Evening
Post* and for the next twenty-five years almost all
his books appeared first in this paper. In 1906 he
wrote some lyrics to music by Jerome Kern, and
some years later he formed a partnership with
Guy Bolton, which resulted in a number of shows
and straight plays. Mr Wodehouse worked at
plays with George Grossmith and Ian Hay, and
has made some adaptations. He has written over
seventy books, several of which are available in
Penguins.

P. G. Wodehouse

Psmith in the City

Penguin Books

Penguin Books Ltd, Harmondsworth,
Middlesex, England
Penguin Books Inc., 7110 Ambassador Road,
Baltimore, Maryland 21207, U.S.A.
Penguin Books Australia Ltd, Ringwood,
Victoria, Australia
Penguin Books Canada Ltd, 41 Steelcase Road West,
Markham, Ontario, Canada
Penguin Books (N.Z.) Ltd, 182–190 Wairau Road,
Auckland 10, New Zealand

First published by A. & C. Black 1910
Published in Penguin Books 1970
Reprinted 1971, 1975

Made and printed in Great Britain by
Cox & Wyman Ltd,
London, Reading and Fakenham
Set in Intertype Times

Several years ago ~ Killarney
I was talking with a woman of there
It had been years
Since I was in Ireland
"How has Ireland changed
in last thirty years?"

to Leslie Havergal Bradshaw

"We have become robots"

all this murder, jingle
of speed, the silent, un-
ed individuality of social order communal
And ultimately we have become robots
is a being.

When universally become a person
of robot, I quiet. And into silence

The robots were not happy

They are never happy
They don't smile. They gesticulate. They work
— I have known now they are self-repeated!

And no surgeon
the very capable oncologists
That no ev the personality
is if I am a friend by
non person "a patient" a they the anguishing
I ap ar are aloud to thin cancer.
Zero compassion, why a an art!

Zero tenderness

Zero humanity
They don't smile, their eyes are unroles
they are "professionals"

In our society
old age is a crime
We dump the old in ... asylums
of solitude
at all these "nursing" homes.

Cancer enormous death
and instead of warmth, tenderness, dignity, sunshine
and love —

Capek knew this
Kippen knew this

And I know this

I refuse to be merely a patient
I refuse to ... human being
I am me
I ... the world
I love birds, cats, travel, the sea
I ... left a ... I will die ...
I ... ... I will ... die
& love my ... as a human being

I refuse to be a robot ...
like Wodehouse's Psmith

I refuse to be a slot
like Melville's ...

I am a bird
I fly I sing I ... I love
I ... ... or I cage
... ... I will die
I turn ... the caged bird
... Sing. I

Contents

1. Mr Bickersdyke Walks behind the Bowler's Arm

Considering what a prominent figure Mr John Bickersdyke was to be in Mike Jackson's life, it was only appropriate that he should make a dramatic entry into it. This he did by walking behind the bowler's arm when Mike had scored ninety-eight, causing him thereby to be clean bowled by a long-hop.

It was the last day of the Ilsworth cricket week, and the house team were struggling hard on a damaged wicket. During the first two matches of the week all had been well. Warm sunshine, true wickets, tea in the shade of the trees. But on the Thursday night, as the team champed their dinner contentedly after defeating the Incogniti by two wickets, a pattering of rain made itself heard upon the windows. By bedtime it had settled to a steady downpour. On Friday morning, when the team of the local regiment arrived in their brake, the sun was shining once more in a watery, melancholy way, but play was not possible before lunch. After lunch the bowlers were in their element. The regiment, winning the toss, put together a hundred and thirty, due principally to a last wicket stand between two enormous corporals, who swiped at everything and had luck enough for two whole teams. The house team followed with seventy-eight, of which Psmith, by his usual golf methods, claimed thirty. Mike, who had gone in first as the star bat of the side, had been run out with great promptitude off the first ball of the innings, which his partner had hit in the immediate neighbourhood of point. At close of play the regiment had made five without loss. This, on the Saturday morning, helped by another shower of rain which made the wicket easier for the moment, they had increased to a hundred and forty-eight, leaving the house just two hundred to make on a pitch which looked as if it were made of linseed.

It was during this week that Mike had first made the acquaintance of Psmith's family. Mr Smith had moved from

Shropshire, and taken Ilsworth Hall in a neighbouring county. This he had done, as far as could be ascertained, simply because he had a poor opinion of Shropshire cricket. And just at the moment cricket happened to be the pivot of his life.

'My father,' Psmith had confided to Mike, meeting him at the station in the family motor on the Monday, 'is a man of vast but volatile brain. He has not that calm, dispassionate outlook on life which marks your true philosopher, such as myself. I – '

'I say,' interrupted Mike, eyeing Psmith's movements with apprehension, 'you aren't going to drive, are you?'

'Who else? As I was saying, I am like some contented spectator of a Pageant. My pater wants to jump in and stage-manage. He is a man of hobbies. He never has more than one at a time, and he never has that long. But while he has it, it's all there. When I left the house this morning he was all for cricket. But by the time we get to the ground he may have chucked cricket and taken up the Territorial Army. Don't be surprised if you find the wicket being dug up into trenches, when we arrive, and the pro. moving in echelon towards the pavilion. No,' he added, as the car turned into the drive, and they caught a glimpse of white flannels and blazers in the distance, and heard the sound of bat meeting ball, 'cricket seems still to be topping the bill. Come along, and I'll show you your room. It's next to mine, so that, if brooding on Life in the still hours of the night, I hit on any great truth, I shall pop in and discuss it with you.'

While Mike was changing, Psmith sat on his bed, and continued to discourse.

'I suppose you're going to the 'Varsity?' he said.

'Rather,' said Mike, lacing his boots. 'You are, of course? Cambridge, I hope. I'm going to King's.'

'Between ourselves,' confided Psmith, 'I'm dashed if I know what's going to happen to me. I am the thingummy of what's-its-name.'

'You look it,' said Mike, brushing his hair.

'Don't stand there cracking the glass,' said Psmith. 'I tell you I am practically a human three-shies-a-penny ball. My father is poising me lightly in his hand, preparatory to flinging me at one of the milky cocos of Life. Which one he'll aim at I don't know. The least thing fills him with a whirl of new views as to my future. Last week we were out shooting together, and he said that the life of the gentleman-farmer was the most manly and independent on earth, and that he had a good mind to start me on that. I pointed out that lack of early training had rendered me unable to distinguish between a threshing-machine and a mangel-wurzel, so he chucked that. He has now worked round to Commerce. It seems that a blighter of the name of Bickersdyke is coming here for the week-end next Saturday. As far as I can say without searching the Newgate Calendar, the man Bickersdyke's career seems to have been as follows. He was at school with my pater, went into the City, raked in a certain amount of doubloons – probably dishonestly – and is now a sort of Captain of Industry, manager of some bank or other, and about to stand for Parliament. The result of these excesses is that my pater's imagination has been fired, and at time of going to press he wants me to imitate Comrade Bickersdyke. However, there's plenty of time. That's one comfort. He's certain to change his mind again. Ready? Then suppose we filter forth into the arena?'

Out on the field Mike was introduced to the man of hobbies. Mr Smith, senior, was a long, earnest-looking man who might have been Psmith in a grey wig but for his obvious energy. He was as wholly on the move as Psmith was wholly statuesque. Where Psmith stood like some dignified piece of sculpture, musing on deep questions with a glassy eye, his father would be trying to be in four places at once. When Psmith presented Mike to him, he shook hands warmly with him and started a sentence, but broke off in the middle of both performances to dash wildly in the direction of the pavilion in an endeavour to catch an impossible catch some thirty yards away. The impetus so gained carried him on towards Bagley, the Ilsworth Hall ground-man, with whom a moment later he was carrying on an animated discussion as to whether he had or had not seen a dandelion on the field that morning. Two minutes afterwards he had skimmed away again. Mike, as he watched him, began to appreciate Psmith's reasons for feeling some doubt as to what would be his future walk in life.

At lunch that day Mike sat next to Mr Smith, and improved his acquaintance with him; and by the end of the week they were on excellent terms. Psmith's father had Psmith's gift of getting on well with people.

On this Saturday, as Mike buckled on his pads, Mr Smith bounded up, full of advice and encouragement.

'My boy,' he said, 'we rely on you. These others' – he indicated with a disparaging wave of the hand the rest of the team, who were visible through the window of the changing-room – 'are all very well. Decent club bats. Good for a few on a billiard-table. But you're our hope on a wicket like this. I have studied cricket all my life' – till that summer it is improbable that Mr Smith had ever handled a bat – 'and I know a first-class batsman when I see one. I've seen your brothers play. Pooh, you're better than any of them. That century of yours against the Green Jackets was a wonderful innings, wonderful. Now look here, my boy. I want you to be careful. We've a lot of runs to make, so we mustn't take any risks. Hit plenty of boundaries, of course, but be careful. Careful. Dash it, there's a youngster trying to climb up the elm. He'll break his neck. It's young Giles, my keeper's boy. Hi! Hi, there!'

He scudded out to avert the tragedy, leaving Mike to digest his expert advice on the art of batting on bad wickets.

Possibly it was the excellence of this advice which induced Mike to play what was, to date, the best innings of his life. There are moments when the batsman feels an almost superhuman fitness. This came to Mike now. The sun had begun to shine strongly. It made the wicket more difficult, but it added a cheerful touch to the scene. Mike felt calm and masterful. The bowling had no terrors for him. He scored nine off his first over and seven off his second, half-way through which he lost his partner. He was to undergo a similar bereavement several times that afternoon, and at frequent intervals. However simple the bowling might seem to him, it had enough sting in it to worry the rest of the team considerably. Batsmen came and went at the other end with such rapidity that it seemed hardly worth while their troubling to come in at all. Every now and then one would give promise of better things by lifting the slow bowler into the pavilion or over the boundary, but it always happened that a similar stroke, a few balls later, ended in an easy catch. At five o'clock the Ilsworth score was eighty-one for seven wickets, last man nought, Mike not out fifty-nine. As most of the house team, including Mike, were dispersing to their homes or were due for visits at other houses that night, stumps were to be drawn at six. It was obvious that they could not hope to win.

Number nine on the list, who was Bagley, the ground-man, went in with instructions to play for a draw, and minute advice from Mr Smith as to how he was to do it. Mike had now begun to score rapidly, and it was not to be expected that he could change his game; but Bagley, a dried-up little man of the type which bowls for five hours on a hot August day without exhibiting any symptoms of fatigue, put a much-bound bat stolidly in front of every ball he received; and the Hall's prospects of saving the game grew brighter.

At a quarter to six the professional left, caught at very silly point for eight. The score was a hundred and fifteen, of which Mike had made eighty-five.

A lengthy young man with yellow hair, who had done some good fast bowling for the Hall during the week, was the next man in. In previous matches he had hit furiously at everything, and against the Green Jackets had knocked up forty in twenty minutes while Mike was putting the finishing touches to his century. Now, however, with his host's warning ringing in his ears, he adopted the unspectacular, or Bagley, style of play. His manner of dealing with the ball was that of one playing croquet. He patted it gingerly back to the bowler when it was straight, and left it icily alone when it was off the wicket. Mike, still in the brilliant vein, clumped a half-volley past point to the boundary, and with highly scientific late cuts and glides brought his score to ninety-eight. With Mike's score at this, the total at a hundred and thirty, and the hands of the clock at five minutes to six, the yellow-haired croquet exponent fell, as Bagley had fallen, a victim to silly point, the ball being the last of the over.

Mr Smith, who always went in last for his side, and who so far had not received a single ball during the week, was down the pavilion steps and half-way to the wicket before the retiring batsman had taken half a dozen steps.

'Last over,' said the wicket-keeper to Mike. 'Any idea how many you've got? You must be near your century, I should think.'

'Ninety-eight,' said Mike. He always counted his runs.

'By Jove, as near as that? This is something like a finish.'

Mike left the first ball alone, and the second. They were too wide of the off-stump to be hit at safely. Then he felt a thrill as the third ball left the bowler's hand. It was a long-hop. He faced square to pull it.

13

And at that moment Mr John Bickersdyke walked into his life across the bowling-screen.

He crossed the bowler's arm just before the ball pitched. Mike lost sight of it for a fraction of a second, and hit wildly. The next moment his leg stump was askew; and the Hall had lost the match.

'I'm sorry,' he said to Mr Smith. 'Some silly idiot walked across the screen just as the ball was bowled.'

'What!' shouted Mr Smith. 'Who was the fool who walked behind the bowler's arm?' he yelled appealingly to Space.

'Here he comes, whoever he is,' said Mike.

A short, stout man in a straw hat and a flannel suit was walking towards them. As he came nearer Mike saw that he had a hard, thin-lipped mouth, half-hidden by a rather ragged moustache, and that behind a pair of gold spectacles were two pale and slightly protruding eyes, which, like his mouth, looked hard.

'How are you, Smith,' he said.

'Hullo, Bickersdyke.' There was a slight internal struggle, and then Mr Smith ceased to be the cricketer and became the host. He chatted amiably to the new-comer.

'You lost the game, I suppose,' said Mr Bickersdyke.

The cricketer in Mr Smith came to the top again, blended now, however, with the host. He was annoyed, but restrained in his annoyance.

'I say, Bickersdyke, you know, my dear fellow,' he said complainingly, 'you shouldn't have walked across the screen. You put Jackson off, and made him get bowled.'

'The screen?'

'That curious white object,' said Mike. 'It is not put up merely as an ornament. There's a sort of rough idea of giving the batsman a chance of seeing the ball, as well. It's a great help to him when people come charging across it just as the bowler bowls.'

Mr Bickersdyke turned a slightly deeper shade of purple, and was about to reply, when what sporting reporters call 'the veritable ovation' began.

Quite a large crowd had been watching the game, and they expressed their approval of Mike's performance.

There is only one thing for a batsman to do on these occasions. Mike ran into the pavilion, leaving Mr Bickersdyke standing.

2. Mike Hears Bad News

It seemed to Mike, when he got home, that there was a touch of gloom in the air. His sisters were as glad to see him as ever. There was a good deal of rejoicing going on among the female Jacksons because Joe had scored his first double century in first-class cricket. Double centuries are too common, nowadays, for the papers to take much notice of them; but, still, it is not everybody who can make them, and the occasion was one to be marked. Mike had read the news in the evening paper in the train, and had sent his brother a wire from the station, congratulating him. He had wondered whether he himself would ever achieve the feat in first-class cricket. He did not see why he should not. He looked forward through a long vista of years of county cricket. He had a birth qualification for the county in which Mr Smith had settled, and he had played for it once already at the beginning of the holidays. His *début* had not been sensational, but it had been promising. The fact that two members of the team had made centuries, and a third seventy odd, had rather eclipsed his own twenty-nine not out; but it had been a faultless innings, and nearly all the papers had said that here was yet another Jackson, evidently well up to the family standard, who was bound to do big things in the future.

The touch of gloom was contributed by his brother Bob to a certain extent, and by his father more noticeably. Bob looked slightly thoughtful. Mr Jackson seemed thoroughly worried.

Mike approached Bob on the subject in the billiard-room after dinner. Bob was practising cannons in rather a listless way.

'What's up, Bob?' asked Mike.

Bob laid down his cue.

'I'm hanged if I know,' said Bob. 'Something seems to be. Father's worried about something.'

'He looked as if he'd got the hump rather at dinner.'

'I only got here this afternoon, about three hours before you did. I had a bit of a talk with him before dinner. I can't make out what's up. He seemed awfully keen on my finding something to do now I've come down from Oxford. Wanted to know whether I couldn't get a tutoring job or a mastership at some school next term. I said I'd have a shot. I don't see what all the hurry's about, though. I was hoping he'd give me a bit of travelling on the Continent somewhere before I started in.'

'Rough luck,' said Mike. 'I wonder why it is. Jolly good about Joe, wasn't it? Let's have fifty up, shall we?'

Bob's remarks had given Mike no hint of impending disaster. It seemed strange, of course, that his father, who had always been so easy-going, should have developed a hustling Get On or Get Out spirit, and be urging Bob to Do It Now; but it never occurred to him that there could be any serious reason for it. After all, fellows had to start working some time or other. Probably his father had merely pointed this out to Bob, and Bob had made too much of it.

Half-way through the game Mr Jackson entered the room, and stood watching in silence.

'Want a game, father?' asked Mike.

'No, thanks, Mike. What is it? A hundred up?'

'Fifty.'

'Oh, then you'll be finished in a moment. When you are, I wish you'd just look into the study for a moment, Mike. I want to have a talk with you.'

'Rum,' said Mike, as the door closed. 'I wonder what's up?'

For a wonder his conscience was free. It was not as if a bad school-report might have arrived in his absence. His Sedleigh report had come at the beginning of the holidays, and had been, on the whole, fairly decent – nothing startling either way. Mr Downing, perhaps through remorse at having harried Mike to such an extent during the Sammy episode, had exercised a studied moderation in his remarks. He had let Mike down far more easily than he really deserved. So it could not be a report that was worrying Mr Jackson. And there was nothing else on his conscience.

Bob made a break of sixteen, and ran out. Mike replaced his cue, and walked to the study.

His father was sitting at the table. Except for the very important fact that this time he felt that he could plead Not Guilty on every possible charge, Mike was struck by the resemblance in the general arrangement of the scene to that painful ten minutes at the end of the previous holidays, when his father had announced his intention of taking him away from Wrykyn and sending him to Sedleigh. The resemblance was increased by the fact that, as Mike entered, Mr Jackson was kicking at the waste-paper basket – a thing which with him was an infallible sign of mental unrest.

'Sit down, Mike,' said Mr Jackson. 'How did you get on during the week?'

'Topping. Only once out under double figures. And then I was run out. Got a century against the Green Jackets, seventy-one against the Incogs, and today I made ninety-eight on a beast of a wicket, and only got out because some silly goat of a chap – '

He broke off. Mr Jackson did not seem to be attending. There was a silence. Then Mr Jackson spoke with an obvious effort.

'Look here, Mike, we've always understood one another, haven't we?'

'Of course we have.'

'You know I wouldn't do anything to prevent you having a good time, if I could help it. I took you away from Wrykyn, I know, but that was a special case. It was necessary. But I understand perfectly how keen you are to go to Cambridge, and I wouldn't stand in the way for a minute, if I could help it.'

Mike looked at him blankly. This could only mean one thing. He was not to go to the 'Varsity. But why? What had happened? When he had left for the Smith's cricket week, his name had been down for King's, and the whole thing settled. What could have happened since then?'

'But I can't help it,' continued Mr Jackson.

'Aren't I going up to Cambridge, father?' stammered Mike.

'I'm afraid not, Mike. I'd manage it if I possibly could. I'm just as anxious to see you get your Blue as you are to get it. But it's kinder to be quite frank. I can't afford to send you to Cambridge. I won't go into details which you would not understand; but I've lost a very large sum of money since I saw you last. So large that we shall have to economize in every way. I shall let this house and take a much smaller one. And you and Bob, I'm afraid, will have to start earning your living. I know it's a terrible disappointment to you, old chap.'

'Oh, that's all right,' said Mike thickly. There seemed to be something sticking in his throat, preventing him from speaking.

'If there was any possible way –'

'No, it's all right, father, really. I don't mind a bit. It's awfully rough luck on you losing all that.'

There was another silence. The clock ticked away energetically on the mantelpiece, as if glad to make itself heard at last. Outside, a plaintive snuffle made itself heard. John, the bull-dog, Mike's inseparable companion, who had followed him to the study, was getting tired of waiting on the mat. Mike got up and opened the door. John lumbered in.

The movement broke the tension.

'Thanks, Mike,' said Mr Jackson, as Mike started to leave the room, 'you're a sportsman.'

3. The New Era Begins

Details of what were in store for him were given to Mike next morning. During his absence at Ilsworth a vacancy had been got for him in that flourishing institution, the New Asiatic Bank; and he was to enter upon his duties, whatever they might be, on the Tuesday of the following week. It was short notice, but banks have a habit of swallowing their victims rather abruptly. Mike remembered the case of Wyatt, who had had just about the same amount of time in which to get used to the prospect of Commerce.

On the Monday morning a letter arrived from Psmith. Psmith was still perturbed. 'Commerce,' he wrote, 'continues to boom. My pater referred to Comrade Bickersdyke last night as a Merchant Prince. Comrade B. and I do not get on well together. Purely for his own good, I drew him aside yesterday and explained to him at great length the frightfulness of walking across the bowling-screen. He seemed restive, but I was firm. We parted rather with the Distant Stare than the Friendly Smile. But I shall persevere. In many ways the casual observer would say that he was hopeless. He is a poor performer at Bridge, as I was compelled to hint to him on Saturday night. His eyes have no animated sparkle of intelligence. And the cut of his clothes jars my sensitive soul to its foundations. I don't wish to speak ill of a man behind his back, but I must confide in you, as my Boyhood's Friend, that he wore a made-up tie at dinner. But no more of a painful subject. I am working away at him with a brave smile. Sometimes I think that I am succeeding. Then he seems to slip back again. However,' concluded the letter, ending on an optimistic note, 'I think that I shall make a man of him yet – some day.'

Mike re-read this letter in the train that took him to London. By this time Psmith would know that his was not the only case in which Commerce was booming. Mike had written to him by return, telling him of the disaster which had befallen the house

19

of Jackson. Mike wished he could have told him in person, for Psmith had a way of treating unpleasant situations as if he were merely playing at them for his own amusement. Psmith's attitude towards the slings and arrows of outrageous Fortune was to regard them with a bland smile, as if they were part of an entertainment got up for his express benefit.

Arriving at Paddington, Mike stood on the platform, waiting for his box to emerge from the luggage-van, with mixed feelings of gloom and excitement. The gloom was in the larger quantities, perhaps, but the excitement was there, too. It was the first time in his life that he had been entirely dependent on himself. He had crossed the Rubicon. The occasion was too serious for him to feel the same helplessly furious feeling with which he had embarked on life at Sedleigh. It was possible to look on Sedleigh with quite a personal enmity. London was too big to be angry with. It took no notice of him. It did not care whether he was glad to be there or sorry, and there was no means of making it care. That is the peculiarity of London. There is a sort of cold unfriendliness about it. A city like New York makes the new arrival feel at home in half an hour; but London is a specialist in what Psmith in his letter had called the Distant Stare. You have to buy London's good-will.

Mike drove across the Park to Victoria, feeling very empty and small. He had settled on Dulwich as the spot to get lodgings, partly because, knowing nothing about London, he was under the impression that rooms anywhere inside the four-mile radius were very expensive, but principally because there was a school at Dulwich, and it would be a comfort being near a school. He might get a game of fives there sometimes, he thought, on a Saturday afternoon, and, in the summer, occasional cricket.

Wandering at a venture up the asphalt passage which leads from Dulwich station in the direction of the College, he came out into Acacia Road. There is something about Acacia Road which inevitably suggests furnished apartments. A child could tell at a glance that it was bristling with bed-sitting rooms.

Mike knocked at the first door over which a card hung.

There is probably no more depressing experience in the world than the process of engaging furnished apartments. Those who let furnished apartments seem to take no joy in the act. Like Pooh-Bah, they do it, but it revolts them.

In answer to Mike's knock, a female person opened the door. In appearance she resembled a pantomime 'dame', inclining towards the restrained melancholy of Mr Wilkie Bard rather than the joyous abandon of Mr George Robey. Her voice she had modelled on the gramophone. Her most recent occupation seemed to have been something with a good deal of yellow soap in it. As a matter of fact – there are no secrets between our readers and ourselves – she had been washing a shirt. A useful occupation, and an honourable, but one that tends to produce a certain homeliness in the appearance.

She wiped a pair of steaming hands on her apron, and regarded Mike with an eye which would have been markedly expressionless in a boiled fish.

'Was there anything?' she asked.

Mike felt that he was in for it now. He had not sufficient ease of manner to back gracefully away and disappear, so he said that there was something. In point of fact, he wanted a bed-sitting room.

'Orkup stays,' said the pantomime dame. Which Mike interpreted to mean, would he walk upstairs?

The procession moved up a dark flight of stairs until it came to a door. The pantomime dame opened this, and shuffled through. Mike stood in the doorway, and looked in.

It was a repulsive room. One of those characterless rooms which are only found in furnished apartments. To Mike, used to the comforts of his bedroom at home and the cheerful simplicity of a school dormitory, it seemed about the most dismal spot he had ever struck. A sort of Sargasso Sea among bedrooms.

He looked round in silence. Then he said: 'Yes.' There did not seem much else to say.

'It's a nice room,' said the pantomime dame. Which was a black lie. It was not a nice room. It never had been a nice room. And it did not seem at all probable that it ever would be a nice room. But it looked cheap. That was the great thing. Nobody could have the assurance to charge much for a room like that. A landlady with a conscience might even have gone to the length of paying people some small sum by way of compensation to them for sleeping in it.

'About what?' queried Mike. Cheapness was the great consideration. He understood that his salary at the bank would be about four pounds ten a month, to begin with, and his father was allowing him five pounds a month. One does not do things *en prince* on a hundred and fourteen pounds a year.

The pantomime dame became slightly more animated. Prefacing her remarks by a repetition of her statement that it was a nice room, she went on to say that she could 'do' it at seven and sixpence per week 'for him' – giving him to understand, presumably, that, if the Shah of Persia or Mr Carnegie ever applied for a night's rest, they would sigh in vain for such easy terms. And that included lights. Coals were to be looked on as an extra. 'Sixpence a scuttle.' Attendance was thrown in.

Having stated these terms, she dribbled a piece of fluff under the bed, after the manner of a professional Association footballer, and relapsed into her former moody silence.

Mike said he thought that would be all right. The pantomime dame exhibited no pleasure.

' 'Bout meals?' she said. 'You'll be wanting breakfast. Bacon, aigs, an' that, I suppose?'

Mike said he supposed so.

'That'll be extra,' she said. 'And dinner? A chop, or a nice steak?'

Mike bowed before this original flight of fancy. A chop or a nice steak seemed to be about what he might want.

'That'll be extra,' said the pantomime dame in her best Wilkie Bard manner.

Mike said yes, he supposed so. After which, having put down seven and sixpence, one week's rent in advance, he was presented with a grubby receipt and an enormous latchkey, and the *séance* was at an end.

Mike wandered out of the house. A few steps took him to the railings that bounded the College grounds. It was late August, and the evenings had begun to close in. The cricket-field looked very cool and spacious in the dim light, with the school buildings looming vague and shadowy through the slight mist. The little gate by the railway bridge was not locked. He went in, and walked slowly across the turf towards the big clump of trees which marked the division between the cricket and football fields. It was all very pleasant and soothing after the pantomime dame and her stuffy bed-sitting room. He sat down on a bench beside the second eleven telegraph-board, and looked across the ground at the pavilion. For the first time that day he began to feel really home-sick. Up till now the excitement of a strange venture had borne him up; but the cricket-field and the pavilion reminded him so sharply of Wrykyn. They brought home to him with a cutting distinctness, the absolute finality of his break with the old order of things. Summers would come and go, matches would be played on this ground with all the glory of big scores and keen finishes; but he was done. 'He was a jolly good bat at school. Top of the Wrykyn averages two years. But didn't do anything after he left. Went into the city or something.' That was what they would say of him, if they didn't quite forget him.

The clock on the tower over the senior block chimed quarter after quarter, but Mike sat on, thinking. It was quite late when he got up, and began to walk back to Acacia Road. He felt cold and stiff and very miserable.

4. First Steps in a Business Career

The City received Mike with the same aloofness with which the more western portion of London had welcomed him on the previous day. Nobody seemed to look at him. He was permitted to alight at St Paul's and make his way up Queen Victoria Street without any demonstration. He followed the human stream till he reached the Mansion House, and eventually found himself at the massive building of the New Asiatic Bank, Limited.

The difficulty now was to know how to make an effective entrance. There was the bank, and here was he. How had he better set about breaking it to the authorities that he had positively arrived and was ready to start earning his four pound ten *per mensem*? Inside, the bank seemed to be in a state of some confusion. Men were moving about in an apparently irresolute manner. Nobody seemed actually to be working. As a matter of fact, the business of a bank does not start very early in the morning. Mike had arrived before things had really begun to move. As he stood near the doorway, one or two panting figures rushed up the steps, and flung themselves at a large book which stood on the counter near the door. Mike was to come to know this book well. In it, if you were an *employé* of the New Asiatic Bank, you had to inscribe your name every morning. It was removed at ten sharp to the accountant's room, and if you reached the bank a certain number of times in the year too late to sign, bang went your bonus.

After a while things began to settle down. The stir and confusion gradually ceased. All down the length of the bank, figures could be seen, seated on stools and writing hieroglyphics in large letters. A benevolent-looking man, with spectacles and a straggling grey beard, crossed the gangway close to where Mike was standing. Mike put the thing to him, as man to man.

'Could you tell me,' he said, 'what I'm supposed to do? I've just joined the bank.' The benevolent man stopped, and looked

24

at him with a pair of mild blue eyes. 'I think, perhaps, that your best plan would be to see the manager,' he said. 'Yes, I should certainly do that. He will tell you what work you have to do. If you will permit me, I will show you the way.'

'It's awfully good of you,' said Mike. He felt very grateful. After his experience of London, it was a pleasant change to find someone who really seemed to care what happened to him. His heart warmed to the benevolent man.

'It feels strange to you, perhaps, at first, Mr –'

'Jackson.'

'Mr Jackson. My name is Waller. I have been in the City some time, but I can still recall my first day. But one shakes down. One shakes down quite quickly. Here is the manager's room. If you go in, he will tell you what to do.'

'Thanks awfully,' said Mike.

'Not at all.' He ambled off on the quest which Mike had interrupted, turning, as he went, to bestow a mild smile of encouragement on the new arrival. There was something about Mr Waller which reminded Mike pleasantly of the White Knight in 'Alice through the Looking-glass.'

Mike knocked at the managerial door, and went in.

Two men were sitting at the table. The one facing the door was writing when Mike went in. He continued to write all the time he was in the room. Conversation between other people in his presence had apparently no interest for him, nor was it able to disturb him in any way.

The other man was talking into a telephone. Mike waited till he had finished. Then he coughed. The man turned round. Mike had thought, as he looked at his back and heard his voice, that something about his appearance or his way of speaking was familiar. He was right. The man in the chair was Mr Bickersdyke, the cross-screen pedestrian.

These reunions are very awkward. Mike was frankly unequal to the situation. Psmith, in his place, would have opened the conversation, and relaxed the tension with some remark on the weather or the state of the crops. Mike merely stood wrapped in silence, as in a garment.

That the recognition was mutual was evident from Mr Bickersdyke's look. But apart from this, he gave no sign of having already had the pleasure of making Mike's acquaintance. He merely stared at him as if he were a blot on the arrangement of the furniture, and said, 'Well?'

The most difficult parts to play in real life as well as on the stage are those in which no 'business' is arranged for the performer. It was all very well for Mr Bickersdyke. He had been 'discovered sitting'. But Mike had had to enter, and he wished now that there was something he could do instead of merely standing and speaking.

'I've come,' was the best speech he could think of. It was not a good speech. It was too sinister. He felt that even as he said it. It was the sort of thing Mephistopheles would have said to Faust by way of opening conversation. And he was not sure, either, whether he ought not to have added, 'Sir.'

Apparently such subtleties of address were not necessary, for Mr Bickersdyke did not start up and shout, 'This language to me!' or anything of that kind. He merely said, 'Oh! And who are you?'

'Jackson,' said Mike. It was irritating, this assumption on Mr Bickersdyke's part that they had never met before.

'Jackson? Ah, yes. You have joined the staff?'

Mike rather liked this way of putting it. It lent a certain dignity to the proceedings, making him feel like some important person for whose services there had been strenuous competition. He seemed to see the bank's directors being reassured by the chairman. ('I am happy to say, gentlemen, that our profits for the past year are £3,000,006-2-2½ – (cheers) – and' – impressively – 'that we have finally succeeded in inducing Mr Mike Jackson – (sensation) – to – er – in fact, to join the staff! (Frantic cheers, in which the chairman joined.')

'Yes,' he said.

Mr Bickersdyke pressed a bell on the table beside him, and picking up a pen, began to write. Of Mike he took no further notice, leaving that toy of Fate standing stranded in the middle of the room.

After a few moments one of the men in fancy dress, whom Mike had seen hanging about the gangway, and whom he afterwards found to be messengers, appeared. Mr Bickersdyke looked up.

'Ask Mr Bannister to step this way,' he said.

The messenger disappeared, and presently the door opened again to admit a shock-headed youth with paper cuff-protectors round his wrists.

'This is Mr Jackson, a new member of the staff. He will take your place in the postage department. You will go into the cash department, under Mr Waller. Kindly show him what he has to do.'

Mike followed Mr Bannister out. On the other side of the door the shock-headed one became communicative.

'Whew!' he said, mopping his brow. 'That's the sort of thing which gives me the pip. When William came and said old Bick wanted to see me, I said to him, "William, my boy, my number is up. This is the sack." I made certain that Rossiter had run me in for something. He's been waiting for a chance to do it for weeks, only I've been as good as gold and haven't given it him. I pity you going into the postage. There's one thing, though. If you can stick it for about a month, you'll get through all right. Men are always leaving for the East, and then you get shunted on into another department, and the next new man goes into the postage. That's the best of this place. It's not like one of those banks where you stay in London all your life. You only have three years here, and then you get your orders, and go to one of the branches in the East, where you're the dickens of a big pot straight away, with a big screw and a dozen native Johnnies under you. Bit of all right, that. I shan't get my orders for another two and a half years and more, worse luck. Still, it's something to look forward to.'

'Who's Rossiter?' asked Mike.

'The head of the postage department. Fussy little brute. Won't leave you alone. Always trying to catch you on the hop. There's one thing, though. The work in the postage is pretty simple. You can't make many mistakes, if you're careful. It's mostly entering letters and stamping them.'

They turned in at the door in the counter, and arrived at a desk which ran parallel to the gangway. There was a high rack running along it, on which were several ledgers. Tall, green-shaded electric lamps gave it rather a cosy look.

As they reached the desk, a little man with short, black whiskers buzzed out from behind a glass screen, where there was another desk.

'Where have you been, Bannister, where have you been? You must not leave your work in this way. There are several letters waiting to be entered. Where have you been?'

'Mr Bickersdyke sent for me,' said Bannister, with the calm triumph of one who trumps an ace.

'Oh! Ah! Oh! Yes, very well. I see. But get to work, get to work. Who is this?'

'This is a new man. He's taking my place. I've been moved on to the cash.'

'Oh! Ah! Is your name Smith?' asked Mr Rossiter, turning to Mike.

Mike corrected the rash guess, and gave his name. It struck him as a curious coincidence that he should be asked if his name were Smith, of all others. Not that it is an uncommon name.

'Mr Bickersdyke told me to expect a Mr Smith. Well, well, perhaps there are two new men. Mr Bickersdyke knows we are short-handed in this department. But, come along, Bannister, come along. Show Jackson what he has to do. We must get on. There is no time to waste.'

He buzzed back to his lair. Bannister grinned at Mike. He was a cheerful youth. His normal expression was a grin.

'That's a sample of Rossiter,' he said. 'You'd think from the fuss he's made that the business of the place was at a standstill till we got to work. Perfect rot! There's never anything to do here till after lunch, except checking the stamps and petty cash, and I've done that ages ago. There are three letters. You may as well enter them. It all looks like work. But you'll find the best way is to wait till you get a couple of dozen or so, and then work them off in a batch. But if you see Rossiter about, then start stamping something or writing something, or he'll run you in for neglecting your job. He's a nut. I'm jolly glad I'm under old Waller now. He's the pick of the bunch. The other heads of departments are all nuts, and Bickersdyke's the nuttiest of the lot. Now, look here. This is all you've got to do. I'll just show you, and then you can manage for yourself. I shall have to be shunting off to my own work in a minute.'

5. The Other Man

As Bannister had said, the work in the postage department was not intricate. There was nothing much to do except enter and stamp letters, and, at intervals, take them down to the post office at the end of the street. The nature of the work gave Mike plenty of time for reflection.

His thoughts became gloomy again. All this was very far removed from the life to which he had looked forward. There are some people who take naturally to a life of commerce. Mike was not of these. To him the restraint of the business was irksome. He had been used to an open-air life, and a life, in its way, of excitement. He gathered that he would not be free till five o'clock, and that on the following day he would come at ten and go at five, and the same every day, except Saturdays and Sundays, all the year round, with a ten days' holiday. The monotony of the prospect appalled him. He was not old enough to know what a narcotic is Habit, and that one can become attached to and interested in the most unpromising jobs. He worked away dismally at his letters till he had finished them. Then there was nothing to do except sit and wait for more.

He looked through the letters he had stamped, and re-read the addresses. Some of them were directed to people living in the country, one to a house which he knew quite well, near to his own home in Shropshire. It made him home-sick, conjuring up visions of shady gardens and country sounds and smells, and the silver Severn gleaming in the distance through the trees. About now, if he were not in this dismal place, he would be lying in the shade in the garden with a book, or wandering down to the river to boat or bathe. That envelope addressed to the man in Shropshire gave him the worst moment he had experienced that day.

The time crept slowly on to one o'clock. At two minutes past Mike awoke from a day-dream to find Mr Waller standing by his side. The cashier had his hat on.

'I wonder,' said Mr Waller, 'if you would care to come out to lunch. I generally go about this time, and Mr Rossiter, I know, does not go out till two. I thought perhaps that, being unused to the City, you might have some difficulty in finding your way about.'

'It's awfully good of you,' said Mike. 'I should like to.'

The other led the way through the streets and down obscure alleys till they came to a chop-house. Here one could have the doubtful pleasure of seeing one's chop in its various stages of evolution. Mr Waller ordered lunch with the care of one to whom lunch is no slight matter. Few workers in the City do regard lunch as a trivial affair. It is the keynote of their day. It in an oasis in a desert of ink and ledgers. Conversation in city office deals, in the morning, with what one is going to have for lunch, and in the afternoon with what one has had for lunch.

At intervals during the meal Mr Waller talked. Mike was content to listen. There was something soothing about the grey-bearded one.

'What sort of a man is Bickersdyke?' asked Mike.

'A very able man. A very able man indeed. I'm afraid he's not popular in the office. A little inclined, perhaps, to be hard on mistakes. I can remember the time when he was quite different. He and I were fellow clerks in Morton and Blather-wick's. He got on better than I did. A great fellow for getting on. They say he is to be the Unionist candidate for Kenningford when the time comes. A great worker, but perhaps not quite the sort of man to be generally popular in an office.'

'He's a blighter,' was Mike's verdict. Mr Waller made no comment. Mike was to learn later that the manager and the cashier, despite the fact that they had been together in less prosperous days – or possibly because of it – were not on very good terms. Mr Bickersdyke was a man of strong prejudices, and he disliked the cashier, whom he looked down upon as one who had climbed to a lower rung of the ladder than he himself had reached.

As the hands of the chop-house clock reached a quarter to two, Mr Waller rose, and led the way back to the office, where they parted for their respective desks. Gratitude for any good turn done to him was a leading characteristic of Mike's nature, and he felt genuinely grateful to the cashier for troubling to seek him out and be friendly to him.

His three-quarters-of-an-hour absence had led to the accumulation of a small pile of letters on his desk. He sat down and began to work them off. The addresses continued to exercise a fascination for him. He was miles away from the office, speculating on what sort of a man J. B. Garside, Esq, was, and whether he had a good time at his house in Worcestershire, when somebody tapped him on the shoulder.

He looked up.

Standing by his side, immaculately dressed as ever, with his eye-glass fixed and a gentle smile on his face, was Psmith.

Mike stared.

'Commerce,' said Psmith, as he drew off his lavender gloves, 'has claimed me for her own. Comrade of old, I, too, have joined this blighted institution.'

As he spoke, there was a whirring noise in the immediate neighbourhood, and Mr Rossiter buzzed out from his den with the *esprit* and animation of a clock-work toy.

'Who's here?' said Psmith with interest, removing his eye-glass, polishing it, and replacing it in his eye.

'Mr Jackson,' exclaimed Mr Rossiter. 'I really must ask you to be good enough to come in from your lunch at the proper time. It was fully seven minutes to two when you returned, and – '

'That little more,' sighed Psmith, 'and how much is it!'

'Who are you?' snapped Mr Rossiter, turning on him.

'I shall be delighted, Comrade – '

'Rossiter,' said Mike, aside.

'Comrade Rossiter. I shall be delighted to furnish you with particulars of my family history. As follows. Soon after the Norman Conquest, a certain Sieur de Psmith grew tired of work – a family failing, alas! – and settled down in this country to live peacefully for the remainder of his life on what he could extract from the local peasantry. He may be described as the founder of the family which ultimately culminated in Me. Passing on – '

Mr Rossiter refused to pass on.

'What are you doing here? What have you come for?'

'Work,' said Psmith, with simple dignity. 'I am now a member of the staff of this bank. Its interests are my interests. Psmith, the individual, ceases to exist, and there springs into being Psmith, the cog in the wheel of the New Asiatic Bank;

Psmith, the link in the bank's chain; Psmith, the Worker. I shall not spare myself,' he proceeded earnestly. 'I shall toil with all the accumulated energy of one who, up till now, has only known what work is like from hearsay. Whose is that form sitting on the steps of the bank in the morning, waiting eagerly for the place to open? It is the form of Psmith, the Worker. Whose is that haggard, drawn face which bends over a ledger long after the other toilers have sped blithely westwards to dine at Lyons' Popular Café? It is the face of Psmith, the Worker.'

'I – ' began Mr Rossiter.

'I tell you,' continued Psmith, waving aside the interruption and tapping the head of the department rhythmically in the region of the second waistcoat-button with a long finger, 'I tell *you*, Comrade Rossiter, that you have got hold of a good man. You and I together, not forgetting Comrade Jackson, the pet of the Smart Set, will toil early and late till we boost up this Postage Department into a shining model of what a Postage Department should be. What that is, at present, I do not exactly know. However. Excursion trains will be run from distant shires to see this Postage Department. American visitors to London will do it before going on to the Tower. And now,' he broke off, with a crisp, businesslike intonation, 'I must ask you to excuse me. Much as I have enjoyed this little chat, I fear it must now cease. The time has come to work. Our trade rivals are getting ahead of us. The whisper goes round, "Rossiter and Psmith are talking, not working," and other firms prepare to pinch our business. Let me Work.'

Two minutes later, Mr Rossiter was sitting at his desk with a dazed expression, while Psmith, perched gracefully on a stool, entered figures in a ledger.

6. Psmith Explains

For the space of about twenty-five minutes Psmith sat in silence, concentrated on his ledger, the picture of the model bank-clerk. Then he flung down his pen, slid from his stool with a satisfied sigh, and dusted his waistcoat. 'A commercial crisis,' he said, 'has passed. The job of work which Comrade Rossiter indicated for me has been completed with masterly skill. The period of anxiety is over. The bank ceases to totter. Are you busy, Comrade Jackson, or shall we chat awhile?'

Mike was not busy. He had worked off the last batch of letters, and there was nothing to do but to wait for the next, or – happy thought – to take the present batch down to the post, and so get out into the sunshine and fresh air for a short time. 'I rather think I'll nip down to the post-office,' said he. 'You couldn't come too, I suppose?'

'On the contrary,' said Psmith, 'I could, and will. A stroll will just restore those tissues which the gruelling work of the last half-hour has wasted away. It is a fearful strain, this commercial toil. Let us trickle towards the post office. I will leave my hat and gloves as a guarantee of good faith. The cry will go round, "Psmith has gone! Some rival institution has kidnapped him!" Then they will see my hat,' – he built up a foundation of ledgers, planted a long ruler in the middle, and hung his hat on it – 'my gloves,' – he stuck two pens into the desk and hung a lavender glove on each – 'and they will sink back swooning with relief. The awful suspense will be over. They will say, "No, he has not gone permanently. Psmith will return. When the fields are white with daisies he'll return." And now, Comrade Jackson, lead me to this picturesque little post-office of yours of which I have heard so much.'

Mike picked up the long basket into which he had thrown the letters after entering the addresses in his ledger, and they moved off down the aisle. No movement came from Mr Rossiter's lair.

Its energetic occupant was hard at work. They could just see part of his hunched-up back.

'I wish Comrade Downing could see us now,' said Psmith. 'He always set us down as mere idlers. Triflers. Butterflies. It would be a wholesome corrective for him to watch us perspiring like this in the cause of Commerce.'

'You haven't told me yet what on earth you're doing here,' said Mike. 'I thought you were going to the 'Varsity. Why the dickens are you in a bank? Your pater hasn't lost his money, has he?'

'No. There is still a tolerable supply of doubloons in the old oak chest. Mine is a painful story.'

'It always is,' said Mike.

'You are very right, Comrade Jackson. I am the victim of Fate. Ah, so you put the little chaps in there, do you?' he said, as Mike, reaching the post-office, began to bundle the letters into the box. 'You seem to have grasped your duties with admirable promptitude. It is the same with me. I fancy we are both born men of Commerce. In a few years we shall be pinching Comrade Bickersdyke's job. And talking of Comrade B. brings me back to my painful story. But I shall never have time to tell it to you during our walk back. Let us drift aside into this tea-shop. We can order a buckwheat cake or a butter-nut, or something equally succulent, and carefully refraining from consuming these dainties, I will tell you all.'

'Right O!' said Mike.

'When last I saw you,' resumed Psmith, hanging Mike's basket on the hat-stand and ordering two portions of porridge, 'you may remember that a serious crisis in my affairs had arrived. My father inflamed with the idea of Commerce had invited Comrade Bickersdyke – '

'When did you know he was a manager here?' asked Mike.

'At an early date. I have my spies everywhere. However, my pater invited Comrade Bickersdyke to our house for the week-end. Things turned out rather unfortunately. Comrade B. resented my purely altruistic efforts to improve him mentally and morally. Indeed, on one occasion he went so far as to call me an impudent young cub, and to add that he wished he had me under him in his bank, where, he asserted, he would knock some of the nonsense out of me. All very painful. I tell you, Comrade Jackson, for the moment it reduced my delicately

34

vibrating ganglions to a mere frazzle. Recovering myself, I made a few blithe remarks, and we then parted. I cannot say that we parted friends, but at any rate I bore him no ill-will. I was still determined to make him a credit to me. My feelings towards him were those of some kindly father to his prodigal son. But he, if I may say so, was fairly on the hop. And when my pater, after dinner the same night, played into his hands by mentioning that he thought I ought to plunge into a career of commerce, Comrade B. was, I gather, all over him. Offered to make a vacancy for me in the bank, and to take me on at once. My pater, feeling that this was the real hustle which he admired so much, had me in, stated his case, and said, in effect, "How do we go?" I intimated that Comrade Bickersdyke was my greatest chum on earth. So the thing was fixed up and here I am. But you are not getting on with your porridge, Comrade Jackson. Perhaps you don't care for porridge? Would you like a finnan haddock, instead? Or a piece of shortbread? You have only to say the word.'

'It seems to me,' said Mike gloomily, 'that we are in for a pretty rotten time of it in this bally bank. If Bickersdyke's got his knife into us, he can make it jolly warm for us. He's got his knife into me all right about that walking-across-the-screen business.'

'True,' said Psmith, 'to a certain extent. It is an undoubted fact that Comrade Bickersdyke will have a jolly good try at making life a nuisance to us; but, on the other hand, I propose, so far as in me lies, to make things moderately unrestful for him, here and there.'

'But you can't,' objected Mike. 'What I mean to say is, it isn't like a school. If you wanted to score off a master at school, you could always rag and so on. But here you can't. How can you rag a man who's sitting all day in a room of his own while you're sweating away at a desk at the other end of the building?'

'You put the case with admirable clearness, Comrade Jackson,' said Psmith approvingly. 'At the hard-headed, common-sense business you sneak the biscuit every time with ridiculous ease. But you do not know all. I do not propose to do a thing in the bank except work. I shall be a model as far as work goes. I shall be flawless. I shall bound to do Comrade Rossiter's bidding like a highly trained performing dog. It is outside the bank, when I have staggered away dazed with toil, that I shall resume my attention to the education of Comrade Bickersdyke.'

'But, dash it all, how can you? You won't see him. He'll go off home, or to his club, or –'

Psmith tapped him earnestly on the chest.

'There, Comrade Jackson,' he said, 'you have hit the bull's-eye, rung the bell, and gathered in the cigar or cocoanut according to choice. He *will* go off to his club. And I shall do precisely the same.'

'How do you mean?'

'It is this way. My father, as you may have noticed during your stay at our stately home of England, is a man of a warm, impulsive character. He does not always do things as other people would do them. He has his own methods. Thus, he has sent me into the City to do the hard-working, bank-clerk act, but at the same time he is allowing me just as large an allowance as he would have given me if I had gone to the 'Varsity. Morever, while I was still at Eton he put my name up for his clubs, the Senior Conservative among others. My pater belongs to four clubs altogether, and in course of time, when my name comes up for election, I shall do the same. Meanwhile, I belong to one, the Senior Conservative. It is a bigger club than the others, and your name comes up for election sooner. About the middle of last month a great yell of joy made the West End of London shake like a jelly. The three thousand members of the Senior Conservative had just learned that I had been elected.'

Psmith paused, and ate some porridge.

'I wonder why they call this porridge,' he observed with mild interest. 'It would be far more manly and straightforward of them to give it its real name. To resume. I have gleaned, from casual chit-chat with my father, that Comrade Bickersdyke also infests the Senior Conservative. You might think that that would make me, seeing how particular I am about whom I mix with, avoid the club. Error. I shall go there every day. If Comrade Bickersdyke wishes to emend any little traits in my character of which he may disapprove, he shall never say that I did not give him the opportunity. I shall mix freely with Comrade Bickersdyke at the Senior Conservative Club. I shall be his constant companion. I shall, in short, haunt the man. By these strenuous means I shall, as it were, get a bit of my own back. And now,' said Psmith, rising, 'it might be as well, perhaps, to return to the bank and resume our commercial duties. I don't know how long you are supposed to be allowed for your little trips to and from the post-office, but, seeing that the distance is about thirty yards, I should say at a venture not more than half an hour. Which is exactly the space of time which has flitted by since we started out on this important expedition. Your devotion to porridge, Comrade Jackson, has led to our spending about twenty-five minutes in this hostelry.'

'Great Scott,' said Mike, 'there'll be a row.'

'Some slight temporary breeze, perhaps,' said Psmith. 'Annoying to men of culture and refinement, but not lasting. My only fear is lest we may have worried Comrade Rossiter at all. I regard Comrade Rossiter as an elder brother, and would not cause him a moment's heart-burning for worlds. However, we shall soon know,' he added, as they passed into the bank and walked up the aisle, 'for there is Comrade Rossiter waiting to receive us in person.'

The little head of the Postage Department was moving restlessly about in the neighbourhood of Psmith's and Mike's desk.

'Am I mistaken,' said Psmith to Mike, 'or is there the merest suspicion of a worried look on our chief's face? It seems to me that there is the slightest soupçon of shadow about that broad, calm brow.'

7. Going into Winter Quarters

There was.

Mr Rossiter had discovered Psmith's and Mike's absence about five minutes after they had left the building. Ever since then, he had been popping out of his lair at intervals of three minutes, to see whether they had returned. Constant disappointment in this respect had rendered him decidedly jumpy. When Psmith and Mike reached the desk, he was a kind of human soda-water bottle. He fizzed over with questions, reproofs, and warnings.

'What does it mean? What does it mean?' he cried. 'Where have you been? Where have you been?'

'Poetry,' said Psmith approvingly.

'You have been absent from your places for over half an hour. Why? Why? Why? Where have you been? Where have you been? I cannot have this. It is preposterous. Where have you been? Suppose Mr Bickersdyke had happened to come round here. I should not have known what to say to him.'

'Never an easy man to chat with, Comrade Bickersdyke,' agreed Psmith.

'You must thoroughly understand that you are expected to remain in your places during business hours.'

'Of course,' said Psmith, 'that makes it a little hard for Comrade Jackson to post letters, does it not?'

'Have you been posting letters?'

'We have,' said Psmith. 'You have wronged us. Seeing our absent places you jumped rashly to the conclusion that we were merely gadding about in pursuit of pleasure. Error. All the while we were furthering the bank's best interests by posting letters.'

'You had no business to leave your place. Jackson is on the posting desk.'

'You are very right,' said Psmith, 'and it shall not occur again. It was only because it was the first day. Comrade Jackson

38

is not used to the stir and bustle of the City. His nerve failed him. He shrank from going to the post-office alone. So I volunteered to accompany him. And,' concluded Psmith, impressively, 'we won safely through. Every letter has been posted.'

'That need not have taken you half an hour.'

'True. And the actual work did not. It was carried through swiftly and surely. But the nerve-strain had left us shaken. Before resuming our more ordinary duties we had to refresh. A brief breathing-space, a little coffee and porridge, and here we are, fit for work once more.'

'If it occurs again, I shall report the matter to Mr Bickersdyke.'

'And rightly so,' said Psmith, earnestly. 'Quite rightly so. Discipline, discipline. That is the cry. There must be no shirking of painful duties. Sentiment must play no part in business. Rossiter, the man, may sympathise, but Rossiter, the Departmental head, must be adamant.'

Mr Rossiter pondered over this for a moment, then went off on a side-issue.

'What is the meaning of this foolery?' he asked, pointing to Psmith's gloves and hat. 'Suppose Mr Bickersdyke had come round and seen them, what should I have said?'

'You would have given him a message of cheer. You would have said, "All is well. Psmith has not left us. He will come back. And Comrade Bickersdyke, relieved, would have – '

'You do not seem very busy, Mr Smith.'

Both Psmith and Mr Rossiter were startled.

Mr Rossiter jumped as if somebody had run a gimlet into him, and even Psmith started slightly. They had not heard Mr Bickersdyke approaching. Mike, who had been stolidly entering addresses in his ledger during the latter part of the conversation, was also taken by surprise.

Psmith was the first to recover. Mr Rossiter was still too confused for speech, but Psmith took the situation in hand.

'Apparently no,' he said, swiftly removing his hat from the ruler. 'In reality, yes. Mr Rossiter and I were just scheming out a line of work for me as you came up. If you had arrived a moment later, you would have found me toiling.'

'H'm. I hope I should. We do not encourage idling in this bank.'

'Assuredly not,' said Psmith warmly. 'Most assuredly not. I would not have it otherwise. I am a worker. A bee, not a drone.

A *Lusitania*, not a limpet. Perhaps I have not yet that grip on my duties which I shall soon acquire; but it is coming. It is coming. I see daylight.'

'H'm. I have only your word for it.' He turned to Mr Rossiter, who had now recovered himself, and was as nearly calm as it was in his nature to be. 'Do you find Mr Smith's work satisfactory, Mr Rossiter?'

Psmith waited resignedly for an outburst of complaint respecting the small matter that had been under discussion between the head of the department and himself; but to his surprise it did not come.

'Oh – ah – quite, quite, Mr Bickersdyke. I think he will very soon pick things up.'

Mr Bickersdyke turned away. He was a conscientious bank manager, and one can only suppose that Mr Rossiter's tribute to the earnestness of one of his employés was gratifying to him. But for that, one would have said that he was disappointed.

'Oh, Mr Bickersdyke,' said Psmith.

The manager stopped.

'Father sent his kind regards to you,' said Psmith benevolently.

Mr Bickersdyke walked off without comment.

'An uncommonly cheery, companionable feller,' murmured Psmith, as he turned to his work.

The first day anywhere, if one spends it in a sedentary fashion, always seemed unending; and Mike felt as if he had been sitting at his desk for weeks when the hour for departure came. A bank's day ends gradually, reluctantly, as it were. At about five there is a sort of stir, not unlike the stir in a theatre when the curtain is on the point of falling. Ledgers are closed with a bang. Men stand about and talk for a moment or two before going to the basement for their hats and coats. Then, at irregular intervals, forms pass down the central aisle and out through the swing doors. There is an air of relaxation over the place, though some departments are still working as hard as ever under a blaze of electric light. Somebody begins to sing, and an instant chorus of protests and maledictions rises from all sides. Gradually, however, the electric lights go out. The procession down the centre aisle becomes more regular; and eventually the place is left to darkness and the night watchman.

The postage department was one of the last to be freed from duty. This was due to the inconsiderateness of the other departments, which omitted to disgorge their letters till the last moment. Mike, as he grew familiar with the work, and began to understand it, used to prowl round the other departments during the afternoon and wrest letters from them, usually receiving with them much abuse for being a nuisance and not leaving honest workers alone. Today, however, he had to sit on till nearly six, waiting for the final batch of correspondence.

Psmith, who had waited patiently with him, though his own work was finished, accompanied him down to the post office and back again to the bank to return the letter basket; and they left the office together.

'By the way,' said Psmith, 'what with the strenuous labours of the bank and the disturbing interviews with the powers that be, I have omitted to ask you where you are digging. Wherever it is, of course you must clear out. It is imperative, in this crisis, that we should be together. I have acquired a quite snug little flat in Clement's Inn. There is a spare bedroom. It shall be yours.'

'My dear chap,' said Mike, 'it's all rot. I can't sponge on you.'

'You pain me, Comrade Jackson. I was not suggesting such a thing. We are business men, hard-headed young bankers. I make you a business proposition. I offer you the post of confidential secretary and adviser to me in exchange for a comfortable home. The duties will be light. You will be required to refuse invitations to dinner from crowned heads, and to listen attentively to my views on Life. Apart from this, there is little to do. So that's settled.'

'It isn't,' said Mike. 'I – '

'You will enter upon your duties tonight. Where are you suspended at present?'

'Dulwich. But, look here – '

'A little more, and you'll get the sack. I tell you the thing is settled. Now, let us hail yon taximeter cab, and desire the stern-faced aristocrat on the box to drive us to Dulwich. We will then collect a few of your things in a bag, have the rest off by train, come back in the taxi, and go and bite a chop at the Carlton. This is a momentous day in our careers, Comrade Jackson. We must buoy ourselves up.'

Mike made no further objections. The thought of that bed-sitting room in Acacia Road and the pantomime dame rose up and killed them. After all, Psmith was not like any ordinary person. There would be no question of charity. Psmith had invited him to the flat in exactly the same spirit as he had invited him to his house for the cricket week.

'You know,' said Psmith, after a silence, as they flitted through the streets in the taximeter, 'one lives and learns. Were you so wrapped up in your work this afternoon that you did not hear my very entertaining little chat with Comrade Bickersdyke, or did it happen to come under your notice? It did? Then I wonder if you were struck by the singular conduct of Comrade Rossiter?'

'I thought it rather decent of him not to give you away to that blighter Bickersdyke.'

'Admirably put. It was precisely that that struck me. He had his opening, all ready made for him, but he refrained from depositing me in the soup. I tell you, Comrade Jackson, my rugged old heart was touched. I said to myself, "There must be good in Comrade Rossiter, after all. I must cultivate him." I shall make it my business to be kind to our Departmental head. He deserves the utmost consideration. His action shone like a good deed in a wicked world. Which it was, of course. From today onwards I take Comrade Rossiter under my wing. We seem to be getting into a tolerably benighted quarter. Are we anywhere near? "Through Darkest Dulwich in a Taximeter." '

The cab arrived at Dulwich station, and Mike stood up to direct the driver. They whirred down Acacia Road. Mike stopped the cab and got out. A brief and somewhat embarrassing interview with the pantomime dame, during which Mike was separated from a week's rent in lieu of notice, and he was in the cab again, bound for Clement's Inn.

His feelings that night differed considerably from the frame of mind in which he had gone to bed the night before. It was partly a very excellent dinner and partly the fact that Psmith's flat, though at present in some disorder, was obviously going to be extremely comfortable, that worked the change. But principally it was due to his having found an ally. The gnawing loneliness had gone. He did not look forward to a career of Commerce with any greater pleasure than before; but there was no doubt that with Psmith, it would be easier to get through the time after office hours. If all went well in the bank he might find that he had not drawn such a bad ticket after all.

8. The Friendly Native

'The first principle of warfare,' said Psmith at breakfast next morning, doling out bacon and eggs with the air of a medieval monarch distributing largesse, 'is to collect a gang, to rope in allies, to secure the cooperation of some friendly native. You may remember that at Sedleigh it was partly the sympathetic cooperation of that record blitherer, Comrade Jellicoe, which enabled us to nip the pro-Spiller movement in the bud. It is the same in the present crisis. What Comrade Jellicoe was to us at Sedleigh, Comrade Rossiter must be in the City. We must make an ally of that man. Once I know that he and I are as brothers, and that he will look with a lenient and benevolent eye on any little shortcomings in my work, I shall be able to devote my attention whole-heartedly to the moral reformation of Comrade Bickersdyke, that man of blood. I look on Comrade Bickersdyke as a bargee of the most pronounced type; and anything I can do towards making him a decent member of Society shall be done freely and ungrudgingly. A trifle more tea, Comrade Jackson?'

'No, thanks,' said Mike. 'I've done. By Jove, Smith, this flat of yours is all right.'

'Not bad,' assented Psmith, 'not bad. Free from squalor to a great extent. I have a number of little objects of *vertu* coming down shortly from the old homestead. Pictures, and so on. It will be by no means un-snug when they are up. Meanwhile, I can rough it. We are old campaigners, we Psmiths. Give us a roof, a few comfortable chairs, a sofa or two, half a dozen cushions, and decent meals, and we do not repine. Reverting once more to Comrade Rossiter – '

'Yes, what about him?' said Mike. 'You'll have a pretty tough job turning him into a friendly native, I should think. How do you mean to start?'

Psmith regarded him with a benevolent eye.

'There is but one way,' he said. 'Do you remember the case

of Comrade Outwood, at Sedleigh? How did we corral him, and become to him practically as long-lost sons?'

'We got round him by joining the Archaeological Society.'

'Precisely,' said Psmith. 'Every man has his hobby. The thing is to find it out. In the case of comrade Rossiter, I should say that it would be either postage stamps, dried seaweed, or Hall Caine. I shall endeavour to find out today. A few casual questions, and the thing is done. Shall we be putting in an appearance at the busy hive now? If we are to continue in the running for the bonus stakes, it would be well to start soon.'

Mike's first duty at the bank that morning was to check the stamps and petty cash. While he was engaged on this task, he heard Psmith conversing affably with Mr Rossiter.

'Good morning,' said Psmith.

'Morning,' replied his chief, doing sleight-of-hand tricks with a bundle of letters which lay on his desk. 'Get on with your work, Psmith. We have a lot before us.'

'Undoubtedly. I am all impatience. I should say that in an institution like this, dealing as it does with distant portions of the globe, a philatelist would have excellent opportunities of increasing his collection. With me, stamp-collecting has always been a positive craze. I – '

'I have no time for nonsense of that sort myself,' said Mr Rossiter. 'I should advise you, if you mean to get on, to devote more time to your work and less to stamps.'

'I will start at once. Dried seaweed, again – '

'Get on with your work, Smith.'

Psmith retired to his desk.

'This,' he said to Mike, 'is undoubtedly something in the nature of a set-back. I have drawn blank. The papers bring out posters, "Psmith Baffled." I must try again. Meanwhile, to work. Work, the hobby of the philosopher and the poor man's friend.'

The morning dragged slowly on without incident. At twelve o'clock Mike had to go out and buy stamps, which he subsequently punched in the punching-machine in the basement, a not very exhilarating job in which he was assisted by one of the bank messengers, who discoursed learnedly on roses during the *séance*. Roses were his hobby. Mike began to see that Psmith had reason in his assumption that the way to every man's heart was through his hobby. Mike made a firm friend of William, the messenger, by displaying an interest and a certain knowledge of roses. At the same time the conversation had the bad effect of leading to an acute relapse in the matter of homesickness. The rose-garden at home had been one of Mike's favourite haunts on a summer afternoon. The contrast between it and the basement of the new Asiatic Bank, the atmosphere of which was far from being roselike, was too much for his feelings. He emerged from the depths, with his punched stamps, filled with bitterness against Fate.

He found Psmith still baffled.

'Hall Caine,' said Psmith regretfully, 'has also proved a frost. I wandered round to Comrade Rossiter's desk just now with a rather brainy excursus on "The Eternal City", and was received with the Impatient Frown rather than the Glad Eye. He was in the middle of adding up a rather tricky column of figures, and my remarks caused him to drop a stitch. So far from winning the man over, I have gone back. There now exists between Comrade Rossiter and myself a certain coldness. Further investigations will be postponed till after lunch.'

The postage department received visitors during the morning. Members of other departments came with letters, among them Bannister. Mr Rossiter was away in the manager's room at the time.

'How are you getting on?' said Bannister to Mike.

'Oh, all right,' said Mike.

'Had any trouble with Rossiter yet?'

'No, not much.'

'He hasn't run you in to Bickersdyke?'

'No.'

'Pardon my interrupting a conversation between old college chums,' said Psmith courteously, 'but I happened to overhear, as I toiled at my desk, the name of Comrade Rossiter.'

Bannister looked somewhat startled. Mike introduced them.

'This is Smith,' he said. 'Chap I was at school with. This is Bannister, Smith, who used to be on here till I came.'

'In this department?' asked Psmith.

'Yes.'

'Then, Comrade Bannister, you are the very man I have been looking for. Your knowledge will be invaluable to us. I have no doubt that, during your stay in this excellently managed department, you had many opportunities of observing Comrade Rossiter?'

'I should jolly well think I had,' said Bannister with a laugh. 'He saw to that. He was always popping out and cursing me about something.'

'Comrade Rossiter's manners are a little restive,' agreed Psmith. 'What used you to talk to him about?'

'What used I to talk to him about?'

'Exactly. In those interviews to which you have alluded, how did you amuse, entertain Comrade Rossiter?'

'I didn't. He used to do all the talking there was.'

Psmith straightened his tie, and clicked his tongue, disappointed.

'This is unfortunate,' he said, smoothing his hair. 'You see, Comrade Bannister, it is this way. In the course of my professional duties, I find myself continually coming into contact with Comrade Rossiter.'

'I bet you do,' said Bannister.

'On these occasions I am frequently at a loss for entertaining conversation. He has no difficulty, as apparently happened in your case, in keeping up his end of the dialogue. The subject of my shortcomings provides him with ample material for speech. I, on the other hand, am dumb. I have nothing to say.'

'I should think that was a bit of a change for you, wasn't it?'

'Perhaps, so,' said Psmith, 'perhaps so. On the other hand, however restful it may be to myself, it does not enable me to secure Comrade Rossiter's interest and win his esteem.'

'What Smith wants to know,' said Mike, 'is whether Rossiter has any hobby of any kind. He thinks, if he has, he might work it to keep in with him.'

Psmith, who had been listening with an air of pleased interest, much as a father would listen to his child prattling for the benefit of a visitor, confirmed this statement.

'Comrade Jackson,' he said, 'has put the matter with his usual admirable clearness. That is the thing in a nutshell. Has Comrade Rossiter any hobby that you know of? Spillikins, brass-rubbing, the Near Eastern Question, or anything like that? I have tried him with postage-stamps (which you'd think, as head of a postage department, he ought to be interested in), and dried seaweed, Hall Caine, but I have the honour to report total failure. The man seems to have no pleasures. What does he do with himself when the day's toil is ended? That giant brain must occupy itself somehow.'

'I don't know,' said Bannister, 'unless it's football. I saw him once watching Chelsea. I was rather surprised.'

'Football,' said Psmith thoughtfully, 'football. By no means a scaly idea. I rather fancy, Comrade Bannister, that you have whanged the nail on the head. Is he strong on any particular team? I mean, have you ever heard him, in the intervals of business worries, stamping on his desk and yelling, "Buck up Cottagers!" or "Lay 'em out, Pensioners!" or anything like that? One moment.' Psmith held up his hand. 'I will get my Sherlock Holmes system to work. What was the other team in the modern gladiatorial contest at which you saw Comrade Rossiter?'

'Manchester United.'

'And Comrade Rossiter, I should say, was a Manchester man.'

'I believe he is.'

'Then I am prepared to bet a small sum that he is nuts on Manchester United. My dear Holmes, how – ! Elementary, my dear fellow, quite elementary. But here comes the lad in person.'

Mr Rossiter turned in from the central aisle through the counter-door, and, observing the conversational group at the postage-desk, came bounding up. Bannister moved off.

'Really, Smith,' said Mr Rossiter, 'you always seem to be talking. I have overlooked the matter once, as I did not wish to get you into trouble so soon after joining; but, really, it cannot go on. I must take notice of it.'

Psmith held up his hand.

'The fault was mine,' he said, with manly frankness. 'Entirely mine. Bannister came in a purely professional spirit to deposit a letter with Comrade Jackson. I engaged him in conversation on the subject of the Football League, and I was just trying to correct his view that Newcastle United were the best team playing, when you arrived.'

'It is perfectly absurd,' said Mr Rossiter, 'that you should waste the bank's time in this way. The bank pays you to work, not to talk about professional football.'

'Just so, just so,' murmured Psmith.

'There is too much talking in this department.'

'I fear you are right.'

'It is nonsense.'

'My own view,' said Psmith, 'was that Manchester United were by far the finest team before the public.'

'Get on with your work, Smith.'

Mr Rossiter stumped off to his desk, where he sat as one in thought.

'Smith,' he said at the end of five minutes.

Psmith slid from his stool, and made his way deferentially towards him.

'Bannister's a fool,' snapped Mr Rossiter.

'So I thought,' said Psmith.

'A perfect fool. He always was.'

Psmith shook his head sorrowfully, as who should say, 'Exit Bannister.'

'There is no team playing today to touch Manchester United.'

'Precisely what I said to Comrade Bannister.'

'Of course. You know something about it.'

'The study of League football,' said Psmith, 'has been my relaxation for years.'

'But we have no time to discuss it now.'

'Assuredly not, sir. Work before everything.'

'Some other time, when – '

' – We are less busy. Precisely.'

Psmith moved back to his seat.

'I fear,' he said to Mike, as he resumed work, 'that as far as Comrade Rossiter's friendship and esteem are concerned, I have to a certain extent landed Comrade Bannister in the bouillon; but it was in a good cause. I fancy we have won through. Half an hour's thoughtful perusal of the "Footballers' Who's Who", just to find out some elementary facts about Manchester United, and I rather think the friendly Native is corralled. And now once more to work. Work, the hobby of the hustler and the deadbeat's dread.'

9. The Haunting of Mr Bickersdyke

Anything in the nature of a rash and hasty move was wholly foreign to Psmith's tactics. He had the patience which is the chief quality of the successful general. He was content to secure his base before making any offensive movement. It was a fortnight before he turned his attention to the education of Mr Bickersdyke. During that fortnight he conversed attractively, in the intervals of work, on the subject of League football in general and Manchester United in particular. The subject is not hard to master if one sets oneself earnestly to it; and Psmith spared no pains. The football editions of the evening papers are not reticent about those who play the game: and Psmith drank in every detail with the thoroughness of the conscientious student. By the end of the fortnight he knew what was the favourite breakfast-food of J. Turnbull; what Sandy Turnbull wore next his skin; and who, in the opinion of Meredith, was England's leading politician. These facts, imparted to and discussed with Mr Rossiter, made the progress of the *entente cordiale* rapid. It was on the eighth day that Mr Rossiter consented to lunch with the Old Etonian. On the tenth he played the host. By the end of the fortnight the flapping of the white wings of Peace over the Postage Department was setting up a positive draught. Mike, who had been introduced by Psmith as a distant relative of Moger, the goalkeeper, was included in the great peace.

'So that now,' said Psmith, reflectively polishing his eye-glass, 'I think that we may consider ourselves free to attend to Comrade Bickersdyke. Our bright little Mancunian friend would no more run us in now than if we were the brothers Turnbull. We are as inside forwards to him.'

The club to which Psmith and Mr Bickersdyke belonged was celebrated for the steadfastness of its political views, the excellence of its cuisine, and the curiously Gorgonzolaesque marble of its main staircase. It takes all sorts to make a world. It took about four thousand of all sorts to make the Senior

Conservative Club. To be absolutely accurate, there were three thousand seven hundred and eighteen members.

To Mr Bickersdyke for the next week it seemed as if there was only one.

There was nothing crude or overdone about Psmith's methods. The ordinary man, having conceived the idea of haunting a fellow clubman, might have seized the first opportunity of engaging him in conversation. Not so Psmith. The first time he met Mr Bickersdyke in the club was on the stairs after dinner one night. The great man, having received practical proof of the excellence of cuisine referred to above, was coming down the main staircase at peace with all men, when he was aware of a tall young man in the 'faultless evening dress' of which the female novelist is so fond, who was regarding him with a fixed stare through an eye-glass. The tall young man, having caught his eye, smiled faintly, nodded in a friendly but patronizing manner, and passed on up the staircase to the library. Mr Bickersdyke sped on in search of a waiter.

As Psmith sat in the library with a novel, the waiter entered, and approached him.

'Beg pardon, sir,' he said. 'Are you a member of this club?'

Psmith fumbled in his pocket and produced his eye-glass, through which he examined the waiter, button by button.

'I am Psmith,' he said simply.

'A member, sir?'

'*The* member,' said Psmith. 'Surely you participated in the general rejoicings which ensued when it was announced that I had been elected? But perhaps you were too busy working to pay any attention. If so, I respect you. I also am a worker. A toiler, not a flatfish. A sizzler, not a squab. Yes, I am a member. Will you tell Mr Bickersdyke that I am sorry, but I have been elected, and have paid my entrance fee and subscription.'

'Thank you, sir.'

The waiter went downstairs and found Mr Bickersdyke in the lower smoking-room.

'The gentleman says he is, sir.'

'H'm,' said the bank-manager. 'Coffee and Benedictine, and a cigar.'

'Yes, sir.'

On the following day Mr Bickersdyke met Psmith in the club three times, and on the day after that seven. Each time the latter's smile was friendly, but patronizing. Mr Bickersdyke began to grow restless.

On the fourth day Psmith made his first remark. The manager was reading the evening paper in a corner, when Psmith sinking gracefully into a chair beside him, caused him to look up.

'The rain keeps off,' said Psmith.

Mr Bickersdyke looked as if he wished his employee would imitate the rain, but he made no reply.

Psmith called a waiter.

'Would you mind bringing me a small cup of coffee?' he said. 'And for you,' he added to Mr Bickersdyke.

'Nothing,' growled the manager.

'And nothing for Mr Bickersdyke.'

The waiter retired. Mr Bickersdyke became absorbed in his paper.

'I see from my morning paper,' said Psmith, affably, 'that you are to address a meeting at the Kenningford Town Hall next week. I shall come and hear you. Our politics differ in some respects, I fear – I incline to the Socialist view – but nevertheless I shall listen to your remarks with great interest, great interest.'

The paper rustled, but no reply came from behind it.

'I heard from father this morning,' resumed Psmith.

Mr Bickersdyke lowered his paper and glared at him.

'I don't wish to hear about your father,' he snapped.

An expression of surprise and pain came over Psmith's face.

'What!' he cried. 'You don't mean to say that there is any coolness between my father and you? I am more grieved than I can say. Knowing, as I do, what a genuine respect my father has for your great talents, I can only think that there must have been some misunderstanding. Perhaps if you would allow me to act as a mediator – '

Mr Bickersdyke put down his paper and walked out of the room.

Psmith found him a quarter of an hour later in the cardroom. He sat down beside his table, and began to observe the play with silent interest. Mr Bickersdyke, never a great performer at the best of times, was so unsettled by the scrutiny that in the deciding game of the rubber he revoked, thereby presenting his opponents with the rubber by a very handsome majority of points. Psmith clicked his tongue sympathetically.

Dignified reticence is not a leading characteristic of the bridge-player's manner at the Senior Conservative Club on occasions like this. Mr Bickersdyke's partner did not bear his calamity with manly resignation. He gave tongue on the instant. 'What on earth's', and 'Why on earth's' flowed from his mouth like molten lava. Mr Bickersdyke sat and fermented in silence. Psmith clicked his tongue sympathetically throughout.

Mr Bickersdyke lost that control over himself which every member of a club should possess. He turned on Psmith with a snort of frenzy.

'How can I keep my attention fixed on the game when you sit staring at me like a – like a – '

'I am sorry,' said Psmith gravely, 'if my stare falls short in any way of your ideal of what a stare should be; but I appeal to these gentlemen. Could I have watched the game more quietly?'

'Of course not,' said the bereaved partner warmly. 'Nobody could have any earthly objection to your behaviour. It was absolute carelessness. I should have thought that one might have expected one's partner at a club like this to exercise elementary – '

But Mr Bickersdyke had gone. He had melted silently away like the driven snow.

Psmith took his place at the table.

'A somewhat nervous excitable man, Mr Bickersdyke, I should say,' he observed.

'A somewhat dashed, blanked idiot,' emended the bank-manager's late partner. 'Thank goodness he lost as much as I did. That's some light consolation.'

Psmith arrived at the flat to find Mike still out. Mike had repaired to the Gaiety earlier in the evening to refresh his mind after the labours of the day. When he returned, Psmith was sitting in an armchair with his feet on the mantelpiece, musing placidly on Life.

'Well?' said Mike.

'Well? And how was the Gaiety? Good show?'

'Jolly good. What about Bickersdyke?'

Psmith looked sad.

'I cannot make Comrade Bickersdyke out,' he said. 'You would think that a man would be glad to see the son of a personal friend. On the contrary, I may be wronging Comrade B., but I should almost be inclined to say that my presence in the Senior Conservative Club tonight irritated him. There was no *bonhomie* in his manner. He seemed to me to be giving a spirited imitation of a man about to foam at the mouth. I did my best to entertain him. I chatted. His only reply was to leave the room. I followed him to the card-room, and watched his very remarkable and brainy tactics at bridge, and he accused me of causing him to revoke. A very curious personality, that of Comrade Bickersdyke. But let us dismiss him from our minds. Rumours have reached me,' said Psmith, 'that a very decent little supper may be obtained at a quaint, old-world eating-house called the Savoy. Will you accompany me thither on a tissue-restoring expedition? It would be rash not to probe these rumours to their foundation, and ascertain their exact truth.'

10. Mr Bickersdyke Addresses His Constituents

It was noted by the observant at the bank next morning that Mr Bickersdyke had something on his mind. William, the messenger, knew it, when he found his respectful salute ignored. Little Briggs, the accountant, knew it when his obsequious but cheerful 'Good morning' was acknowledged only by a 'Morn'' which was almost an oath. Mr Bickersdyke passed up the aisle and into his room like an east wind. He sat down at his table and pressed the bell. Harold, William's brother and co-messenger, entered with the air of one ready to duck if any missile should be thrown at him. The reports of the manager's frame of mind had been circulated in the office, and Harold felt somewhat apprehensive. It was on an occasion very similar to this that George Barstead, formerly in the employ of the New Asiatic Bank in the capacity of messenger, had been rash enough to laugh at what he had taken for a joke of Mr Bickersdyke's, and had been instantly presented with the sack for gross impertinence.

'Ask Mr Smith – ' began the manager. Then he paused. 'No, never mind,' he added.

Harold remained in the doorway, puzzled.

'Don't stand there gaping at me, man,' cried Mr Bickersdyke. 'Go away.'

Harold retired and informed his brother, William, that in his, Harold's, opinion, Mr Bickersdyke was off his chump.

'Off his onion,' said William, soaring a trifle higher in poetic imagery.

'Barmy,' was the terse verdict of Samuel Jakes, the third messenger. 'Always said so.' And with that the New Asiatic Bank staff of messengers dismissed Mr Bickersdyke and proceeded to concentrate themselves on their duties, which consisted principally of hanging about and discussing the prophecies of that modern seer, Captain Coe.

What had made Mr Bickersdyke change his mind so abruptly

was the sudden realization of the fact that he had no case against Psmith. In his capacity of manager of the bank he could not take official notice of Psmith's behaviour outside office hours, especially as Psmith had done nothing but stare at him. It would be impossible to make anybody understand the true inwardness of Psmith's stare. Theoretically, Mr Bickersdyke had the power to dismiss any subordinate of his whom he did not consider satisfactory, but it was a power that had to be exercised with discretion. The manager was accountable for his actions to the Board of Directors. If he dismissed Psmith, Psmith would certainly bring an action against the bank for wrongful dismissal, and on the evidence he would infallibly win it. Mr Bickersdyke did not welcome the prospect of having to explain to the Directors that he had let the shareholders of the bank in for a fine of whatever a discriminating jury cared to decide upon, simply because he had been stared at while playing bridge. His only hope was to catch Psmith doing his work badly.

He touched the bell again, and sent for Mr Rossiter.

The messenger found the head of the Postage Department in conversation with Psmith. Manchester United had been beaten by one goal to nil on the previous afternoon, and Psmith was informing Mr Rossiter that the referee was a robber, who had evidently been financially interested in the result of the game. The way he himself looked at it, said Psmith, was that the thing had been a moral victory for the United. Mr Rossiter said yes, he thought so too. And it was at this moment that Mr Bickersdyke sent for him to ask whether Psmith's work was satisfactory.

The head of the Postage Department gave his opinion without hesitation. Psmith's work was about the hottest proposition he had ever struck. Psmith's work – well, it stood alone. You couldn't compare it with anything. There are no degrees in perfection. Psmith's work was perfect, and there was an end to it.

He put it differently, but that was the gist of what he said.

Mr Bickersdyke observed he was glad to hear it, and smashed a nib by stabbing the desk with it.

It was on the evening following this that the bank-manager was due to address a meeting at the Kenningford Town Hall.

He was looking forward to the event with mixed feelings. He had stood for Parliament once before, several years back, in the North. He had been defeated by a couple of thousand votes, and he hoped that the episode had been forgotten. Not merely because his defeat had been heavy. There was another reason. On that occasion he had stood as a Liberal. He was standing for Kenningford as a Unionist. Of course, a man is at perfect liberty to change his views, if he wishes to do so, but the process is apt to give his opponents a chance of catching him (to use the inspired language of the music-halls) on the bend. Mr Bickersdyke was rather afraid that the light-hearted electors of Kenningford might avail themselves of this chance.

Kenningford, S.E., is undoubtedly by way of being a tough sort of place. Its inhabitants incline to a robust type of humour, which finds a verbal vent in catch phrases and expends itself physically in smashing shop-windows and kicking policemen. He feared that the meeting at the Town Hall might possibly be a trifle rowdy.

All political meetings are very much alike. Somebody gets up and introduces the speaker of the evening, and then the speaker of the evening says at great length what he thinks of the scandalous manner in which the Government is behaving or the iniquitous goings-on of the Opposition. From time to time confederates in the audience rise and ask carefully rehearsed questions, and are answered fully and satisfactorily by the orator. When a genuine heckler interrupts, the orator either ignores him, or says haughtily that he can find him arguments but cannot find him brains. Or, occasionally, when the question is an easy one, he answers it. A quietly conducted political meeting is one of England's most delightful indoor games. When the meeting is rowdy, the audience has more fun, but the speaker a good deal less.

Mr Bickersdyke's introducer was an elderly Scotch peer, an excellent man for the purpose in every respect, except that he possessed a very strong accent.

The audience welcomed that accent uproariously. The electors of Kenningford who really had any definite opinions on politics were fairly equally divided. There were about as many earnest Liberals as there were earnest Unionists. But besides these there was a strong contingent who did not care which side won. These looked on elections as Heaven-sent opportunities for making a great deal of noise. They attended meetings in order to extract amusement from them; and they voted, if they voted at all, quite irresponsibly. A funny story at the expense of one candidate told on the morning of the polling, was quite likely to send these brave fellows off in dozens filling in their papers for the victim's opponent.

There was a solid block of these gay spirits at the back of the hall. They received the Scotch peer with huge delight. He reminded them of Harry Lauder and they said so. They addressed him affectionately as 'Arry', throughout his speech, which was rather long. They implored him to be a pal and sing 'The Saftest of the Family'. Or, failing that, 'I love a lassie'. Finding they could not induce him to do this, they did it themselves. They sang it several times. When the peer, having finished his remarks on the subject of Mr Bickersdyke, at length sat down, they cheered for seven minutes, and demanded an encore.

The meeting was in excellent spirits when Mr Bickersdyke rose to address it.

The effort of doing justice to the last speaker had left the free and independent electors at the back of the hall slightly limp. The bank-manager's opening remarks were received without any demonstration.

Mr Bickersdyke spoke well. He had a penetrating, if harsh, voice, and he said what he had to say forcibly. Little by little the audience came under his spell. When, at the end of a well-turned sentence, he paused and took a sip of water, there was a round of applause, in which many of the admirers of Mr Harry Lauder joined.

He resumed his speech. The audience listened intently. Mr Bickersdyke, having said some nasty things about Free Trade and the Alien Immigrant, turned to the Needs of the Navy and the necessity of increasing the fleet at all costs.

'This is no time for half-measures,' he said. 'We must do our utmost. We must burn our boats – '

'Excuse me,' said a gentle voice.

Mr Bickersdyke broke off. In the centre of the hall a tall figure had risen. Mr Bickersdyke found himself looking at a gleaming eye-glass which the speaker had just polished and inserted in his eye.

The ordinary heckler Mr Bickersdyke would have taken in

his stride. He had got his audience, and simply by continuing and ignoring the interruption, he could have won through in safety. But the sudden appearance of Psmith unnerved him. He remained silent.

'How,' asked Psmith, 'do you propose to strengthen the Navy by burning boats?'

The inanity of the question enraged even the pleasure-seekers at the back.

'Order! Order!' cried the earnest contingent.

'Sit down, fice!' roared the pleasure-seekers.

Psmith sat down with a patient smile.

Mr Bickersdyke resumed his speech. But the fire had gone out of it. He had lost his audience. A moment before, he had grasped them and played on their minds (or what passed for minds down Kenningford way) as on a stringed instrument. Now he had lost his hold.

He spoke on rapidly, but he could not get into his stride. The trivial interruption had broken the spell. His words lacked grip. The dead silence in which the first part of his speech had been received, that silence which is a greater tribute to the speaker than any applause, had given place to a restless medley of little noises; here a cough; there a scraping of a boot along the floor, as its wearer moved uneasily in his seat; in another place a whispered conversation. The audience was bored.

Mr Bickersdyke left the Navy, and went on to more general topics. But he was not interesting. He quoted figures, saw a moment later that he had not quoted them accurately, and instead of carrying on boldly, went back and corrected himself.

'Gow up top!' said a voice at the back of the hall, and there was a general laugh.

Mr Bickersdyke galloped unsteadily on. He condemned the Government. He said they had betrayed their trust.

And then he told an anecdote.

'The Government, gentlemen,' he said, 'achieves nothing worth achieving, and every individual member of the Government takes all the credit for what is done to himself. Their methods remind me, gentlemen, of an amusing experience I had while fishing one summer in the Lake District.'

In a volume entitled 'Three Men in a Boat' there is a story of how the author and a friend go into a riverside inn and see a very large trout in a glass case. They make inquiries about it.

Five men assure them, one by one, that the trout was caught by themselves. In the end the trout turns out to be made of plaster of Paris.

Mr Bickersdyke told that story as an experience of his own while fishing one summer in the Lake District.

It went well. The meeting was amused. Mr Bickersdyke went on to draw a trenchant comparison between the lack of genuine merit in the trout and the lack of genuine merit in the achievements of His Majesty's Government.

There was applause.

When it had ceased, Psmith rose to his feet again.

'Excuse me,' he said.

11. Misunderstood

Mike had refused to accompany Psmith to the meeting that evening, saying that he got too many chances in the ordinary way of business of hearing Mr Bickersdyke speak, without going out of his way to make more. So Psmith had gone off to Kenningford alone, and Mike, feeling too lazy to sally out to any place of entertainment, had remained at the flat with a novel.

He was deep in this, when there was the sound of a key in the latch, and shortly afterwards Psmith entered the room. On Psmith's brow there was a look of pensive care, and also a slight discoloration. When he removed his overcoat, Mike saw that his collar was burst and hanging loose and that he had no tie. On his erstwhile speckless and gleaming shirt front were a number of finger-impressions, of a boldness and clearness of outline which would have made a Bertillon expert leap with joy.

'Hullo!' said Mike dropping his book.

Psmith nodded in silence, went to his bedroom, and returned with a looking-glass. Propping this up on a table, he proceeded to examine himself with the utmost care. He shuddered slightly as his eye fell on the finger-marks; and without a word he went into his bathroom again. He emerged after an interval of ten minutes in sky-blue pyjamas, slippers, and an Old Etonian blazer. He lit a cigarette; and, sitting down, stared pensively into the fire.

'What the dickens have you been playing at?' demanded Mike.

Psmith heaved a sigh.

'That,' he replied, 'I could not say precisely. At one moment it seemed to be Rugby football, at another a jiu-jitsu *séance*. Later, it bore a resemblance to a pantomime rally. However, whatever it was, it was all very bright and interesting. A distinct experience.'

'Have you been scrapping?' asked Mike. 'What happened? Was there a row?'

'There was,' said Psmith, 'in a measure what might be described as a row. At least, when you find a perfect stranger attaching himself to your collar and pulling, you begin to suspect that something of that kind is on the bill.'

'Did they do that?'

Psmith nodded.

'A merchant in a moth-eaten bowler started warbling to a certain extent with me. It was all very trying for a man of culture. He was a man who had, I should say, discovered that alcohol was a food long before the doctors found it out. A good chap, possibly, but a little boisterous in his manner. Well, well.'

Psmith shook his head sadly.

'He got you one on the forehead,' said Mike, 'or somebody did. Tell us what happened. I wish the dickens I'd come with you. I'd no notion there would be a rag of any sort. What did happen?'

'Comrade Jackson,' said Psmith sorrowfully, 'how sad it is in this life of ours to be consistently misunderstood. You know, of course, how wrapped up I am in Comrade Bickersdyke's welfare. You know that all my efforts are directed towards making a decent man of him; that, in short, I am his truest friend. Does he show by so much as a word that he appreciates my labours? Not he. I believe that man is beginning to dislike me, Comrade Jackson.'

'What happened, anyhow? Never mind about Bickersdyke.'

'Perhaps it was mistaken zeal on my part. . . . Well, I will tell you all. Make a long arm for the shovel, Comrade Jackson, and pile on a few more coals. I thank you. Well, all went quite smoothly for a while. Comrade B. in quite good form. Got his second wind, and was going strong for the tape, when a regrettable incident occurred. He informed the meeting, that while up in the Lake country, fishing, he went to an inn and saw a remarkably large stuffed trout in a glass case. He made inquiries, and found that five separate and distinct people had caught – '

'Why, dash it all,' said Mike, 'that's a frightful chestnut.'

Psmith nodded.

'It certainly has appeared in print,' he said. 'In fact I should have said it was rather a well-known story. I was so interested in Comrade Bickersdyke's statement that the thing had happened to himself that, purely out of good-will towards him, I got up and told him that I thought it was my duty, as a friend, to let him know that a man named Jerome had pinched his story, put it in a book, and got money by it. Money, mark you, that should by rights have been Comrade Bickersdyke's. He didn't appear to care much about sifting the matter thoroughly. In fact, he seemed anxious to get on with his speech, and slur the matter over. But, tactlessly perhaps, I continued rather to harp on the thing. I said that the book in which the story had appeared was published in 1889. I asked him how long ago it was that he had been on his fishing tour, because it was important to know in order to bring the charge home against Jerome. Well, after a bit, I was amazed, and pained, too, to hear Comrade Bickersdyke urging certain bravoes in the audience to turn me out. If ever there was a case of biting the hand that fed him. . . . Well, well. . . . By this time the meeting had begun to take sides to some extent. What I might call my party, the Earnest Investigators, were whistling between their fingers, stamping on the floor, and shouting, "Chestnuts!" while the opposing party, the bravoes, seemed to be trying, as I say, to do jui-jitsu tricks with me. It was a painful situation. I know the cultivated man of affairs should have passed the thing off with a short, careless laugh; but, owing to the above-mentioned alcohol-expert having got both hands under my collar, short, careless laughs were off. I was compelled, very reluctantly, to conclude the interview by tapping the bright boy on the jaw. He took the hint, and sat down on the floor. I thought no more of the matter, and was making my way thoughtfully to the exit, when a second man of wrath put the above on my forehead. You can't ignore a thing like that. I collected some of his waistcoat and one of his legs, and hove him with some vim into the middle distance. By this time a good many of the Earnest Investigators were beginning to join in; and it was just there that the affair began to have certain points of resemblance to a pantomime rally. Everybody seemed to be shouting a good deal and hitting everybody else. It was no place for a man of delicate culture, so I edged towards the door, and drifted out. There was a cab in the offing. I boarded it. And, having kicked a vigorous politician in the stomach, as he was endeavouring to climb in too, I drove off home.'

Psmith got up, looked at his forehead once more in the glass, sighed, and sat down again.

'All very disturbing,' he said.

'Great Scott,' said Mike, 'I wish I'd come. Why on earth didn't you tell me you were going to rag? I think you might as well have done. I wouldn't have missed it for worlds.'

Psmith regarded him with raised eyebrows.

'Rag!' he said. 'Comrade Jackson, I do not understand you. You surely do not think that I had any other object in doing what I did than to serve Comrade Bickersdyke? It's terrible how one's motives get distorted in this world of ours.'

'Well,' said Mike, with a grin, 'I know one person who'll jolly well distort your motives, as you call it, and that's Bickersdyke.'

Psmith looked thoughtful.

'True,' he said, 'true. There is that possibility. I tell you, Comrade Jackson, once more that my bright young life is being slowly blighted by the frightful way in which that man misunderstands me. It seems almost impossible to try to do him a good turn without having the action misconstrued.'

'What'll you say to him tomorrow?'

'I shall make no allusion to the painful affair. If I happen to meet him in the ordinary course of business routine, I shall pass some light, pleasant remark – on the weather, let us say, or the Bank rate – and continue my duties.'

'How about if he sends for you, and wants to do the light, pleasant remark business on his own?'

'In that case I shall not thwart him. If he invites me into his private room, I shall be his guest, and shall discuss, to the best of my ability, any topic which he may care to introduce. There shall be no constraint between Comrade Bickersdyke and myself.'

'No, I shouldn't think there would be. I wish I could come and hear you.'

'I wish you could,' said Psmith courteously.

'Still, it doesn't matter much to you. You don't care if you do get sacked.'

Psmith rose.

'In that way possibly, as you say, I am agreeably situated. If the New Asiatic Bank does not require Psmith's services, there are other spheres where a young man of spirit may carve a place for himself. No, what is worrying me, Comrade Jackson, is not the thought of the push. It is the growing fear that Comrade Bickersdyke and I will never thoroughly understand and appreciate one another. A deep gulf lies between us. I do what I can do to bridge it over, but he makes no response. On his side of the gulf building operations appear to be at an entire standstill. That is what is carving these lines of care on my forehead, Comrade Jackson. That is what is painting these purple circles beneath my eyes. Quite inadvertently to be disturbing Comrade Bickersdyke, annoying him, preventing him from enjoying life. How sad this is. Life bulges with these tragedies.'

Mike picked up the evening paper.

'Don't let it keep you awake at night,' he said. 'By the way, did you see that Manchester United were playing this afternoon? They won. You'd better sit down and sweat up some of the details. You'll want them tomorrow.'

'You are very right, Comrade Jackson,' said Psmith, re-seating himself. 'So the Mancunians pushed the bulb into the meshes beyond the uprights no fewer than four times, did they? Bless the dear boys, what spirits they do enjoy, to be sure. Comrade Jackson, do not disturb me. I must concentrate myself. These are deep waters.'

12. In a Nutshell

Mr Bickersdyke sat in his private room at the New Asiatic Bank with a pile of newspapers before him. At least, the casual observer would have said that it was Mr Bickersdyke. In reality, however, it was an active volcano in the shape and clothes of the bank-manager. It was freely admitted in the office that morning that the manager had lowered all records with ease. The staff had known him to be in a bad temper before – frequently; but his frame of mind on all previous occasions had been, compared with his present frame of mind, that of a rather exceptionally good-natured lamb. Within ten minutes of his arrival the entire office was on the jump. The messengers were collected in a pallid group in the basement, discussing the affair in whispers and endeavouring to restore their nerve with about sixpenn'orth of the beverage known as 'unsweetened'. The heads of departments, to a man, had bowed before the storm. Within the space of seven minutes and a quarter Mr Bickersdyke had contrived to find some fault with each of them. Inward Bills was out at an A.B.C. shop snatching a hasty cup of coffee, to pull him together again. Outward Bills was sitting at his desk with the glazed stare of one who has been struck in the thorax by a thunderbolt. Mr Rossiter had been torn from Psmith in the middle of a highly technical discussion of the Manchester United match, just as he was showing – with the aid of a ball of paper – how he had once seen Meredith centre to Sandy Turnbull in a Cup match, and was now leaping about like a distracted grasshopper. Mr Waller, head of the Cash Department, had been summoned to the Presence, and after listening meekly to a rush of criticism, had retired to his desk with the air of a beaten spaniel.

Only one man of the many in the building seemed calm and happy – Psmith.

Psmith had resumed the chat about Manchester United, on Mr Rossiter's return from the lion's den, at the spot where it had been broken off; but, finding that the head of the Postage Department was in no mood for discussing football (or anything else), he had postponed his remarks and placidly resumed his work.

Mr Bickersdyke picked up a paper, opened it, and began searching the columns. He had not far to look. It was a slack season for the newspapers, and his little trouble, which might have received a paragraph in a busy week, was set forth fully in three-quarters of a column.

The column was headed, 'Amusing Heckling'.

Mr Bickersdyke read a few lines, and crumpled the paper up with a snort.

The next he examined was an organ of his own shade of political opinion. It too, gave him nearly a column, headed 'Disgraceful Scene at Kenningford'. There was also a leaderette on the subject.

The leaderette said so exactly what Mr Bickersdyke thought himself that for a moment he was soothed. Then the thought of his grievance returned, and he pressed the bell.

'Send Mr Smith to me,' he said.

William, the messenger, proceeded to inform Psmith of the summons.

Psmith's face lit up.

'I am *always* glad to sweeten the monotony of toil with a chat with Little Clarence,' he said. 'I shall be with him in a moment.'

He cleaned his pen very carefully, placed it beside his ledger, flicked a little dust off his coatsleeve, and made his way to the manager's room.

Mr Bickersdyke received him with the ominous restraint of a tiger crouching for its spring. Psmith stood beside the table with languid grace, suggestive of some favoured confidential secretary waiting for instructions.

A ponderous silence brooded over the room for some moments. Psmith broke it by remarking that the Bank Rate was unchanged. He mentioned this fact as if it afforded him a personal gratification.

Mr Bickersdyke spoke.

'Well, Mr Smith?' he said.

'You wished to see me about something, sir?' inquired Psmith, ingratiatingly.

'You know perfectly well what I wished to see you about. I want to hear your explanation of what occurred last night.'

'May I sit, sir?'

He dropped gracefully into a chair, without waiting for permission, and, having hitched up the knees of his trousers, beamed winningly at the manager.

'A deplorable affair,' he said, with a shake of his head. 'Extremely deplorable. We must not judge these rough, uneducated men too harshly, however. In a time of excitement the emotions of the lower classes are easily stirred. Where you or I would – '

Mr Bickersdyke interrupted.

'I do not wish for any more buffoonery, Mr Smith – '

Psmith raised a pained pair of eyebrows.

'Buffoonery, sir!'

'I cannot understand what made you act as you did last night, unless you are perfectly mad, as I am beginning to think.'

'But, surely, sir, there was nothing remarkable in my behaviour? When a merchant has attached himself to your collar, can you do less than smite him on the other cheek? I merely acted in self-defence. You saw for yourself – '

'You know what I am alluding to. Your behaviour during my speech.'

'An excellent speech,' murmured Psmith courteously.

'Well?' said Mr Bickersdyke.

'It was, perhaps, mistaken zeal on my part, sir, but you must remember that I acted purely from the best motives. It seemed to me – '

'That is enough, Mr Smith. I confess that I am absolutely at a loss to understand you – '

'It is too true, sir,' sighed Psmith.

'You seem,' continued Mr Bickersdyke, warming to his subject, and turning gradually a richer shade of purple, 'you seem to be determined to endeavour to annoy me.' ('No no,' from Psmith.) 'I can only assume that you are not in your right senses. You follow me about in my club – '

'Our club, sir,' murmured Psmith.

'Be good enough not to interrupt me, Mr Smith. You dog my footsteps in my club – '

'Purely accidental, sir. We happen to meet – that is all.'

'You attend meetings at which I am speaking, and behave in a perfectly imbecile manner.'

Psmith moaned slightly.

'It may seem humorous to you, but I can assure you it is extremely bad policy on your part. The New Asiatic Bank is no place for humour, and I think – '

'Excuse me, sir,' said Psmith.

The manager started at the familiar phrase. The plum-colour of his complexion deepened.

'I entirely agree with you, sir,' said Psmith, 'that this bank is no place for humour.'

'Very well, then. You – '

'And I am never humorous in it. I arrive punctually in the morning, and I work steadily and earnestly till my labours are completed. I think you will find, on inquiry, that Mr Rossiter is satisfied with my work.'

'That is neither here nor – '

'Surely, sir,' said Psmith, 'you are wrong? Surely your jurisdiction ceases after office hours? Any little misunderstanding we may have at the close of the day's work cannot affect you officially. You could not, for instance, dismiss me from the service of the bank if we were partners at bridge at the club and I happened to revoke.'

'I can dismiss you, let me tell you, Mr Smith, for studied insolence, whether in the office or not.'

'I bow to superior knowledge,' said Psmith politely, 'but I confess I doubt it. And,' he added, 'there is another point. May I continue to some extent?'

'If you have anything to say, say it.'

Psmith flung one leg over the other, and settled his collar.

'It is perhaps a delicate matter,' he said, 'but it is best to be frank. We should have no secrets. To put my point quite clearly, I must go back a little, to the time when you paid us that very welcome week-end visit at our house in August.'

'If you hope to make capital out of the fact that I have been a guest of your father – '

'Not at all,' said Psmith deprecatingly. 'Not at all. You do not take me. My point is this. I do not wish to revive painful memories, but it cannot be denied that there was, here and there, some slight bickering between us on that occasion. The fault,' said Psmith magnanimously, 'was possibly mine. I may have been too exacting, too capricious. Perhaps so. However, the fact remains that you conceived the happy notion of getting me into this bank, under the impression that, once I was in, you would be able to – if I may use the expression – give me beans. You said as much to me, if I remember. I hate to say it, but don't you think that if you give me the sack, although my work is satisfactory to the head of my department, you will be by way of admitting that you bit off rather more than you could chew? I merely make the suggestion.'

Mr Bickersdyke half rose from his chair.

'You – '

'Just so, just so, but – to return to the main point – don't you? The whole painful affair reminds me of the story of Agesilaus and the Petulant Pterodactyl, which as you have never heard, I will now proceed to relate. Agesilaus – '

Mr Bickersdyke made a curious clucking noise in his throat.

'I am boring you,' said Psmith, with ready tact. 'Suffice it to say that Comrade Agesilaus interfered with the pterodactyl, which was doing him no harm; and the intelligent creature, whose motto was "Nemo me impune lacessit", turned and bit him. Bit him good and hard, so that Agesilaus ever afterwards had a distaste for pterodactyls. His reluctance to disturb them became quite a byword. The Society papers of the period frequently commented upon it. Let us draw the parallel.'

Here Mr Bickersdyke, who had been clucking throughout this speech, essayed to speak; but Psmith hurried on.

'You are Agesilaus,' he said. 'I am the Petulant Pterodactyl. You, if I may say so, butted in of your own free will, and took me from a happy home, simply in order that you might get me into this place under you, and give me beans. But, curiously enough, the major portion of that vegetable seems to be coming to you. Of course, you can administer the push if you like; but, as I say, it will be by way of a confession that your scheme has sprung a leak. Personally,' said Psmith, as one friend to another, 'I should advise you to stick it out. You never know what may happen. At any moment I may fall from my present high standard of industry and excellence; and then you have me, so to speak, where the hair is crisp.'

He paused. Mr Bickersdyke's eyes, which even in their normal state protruded slightly, now looked as if they might fall out at any moment. His face had passed from the plum-coloured stage to something beyond. Every now and then he made the clucking noise, but except for that he was silent. Psmith, having waited for some time for something in the shape of comment or criticism on his remarks, now rose.

'It has been a great treat to me, this little chat,' he said affably, 'but I fear that I must no longer allow purely social enjoyments to interfere with my commercial pursuits. With your permission, I will rejoin my department, where my absence is doubtless already causing comment and possibly dismay. But we shall be meeting at the club shortly, I hope. Good-bye, sir, good-bye.'

He left the room, and walked dreamily back to the Postage Department, leaving the manager still staring glassily at nothing.

13. Mike is Moved On

This episode may be said to have concluded the first act of the commercial drama in which Mike and Psmith had been cast for leading parts. And, as usually happens after the end of an act, there was a lull for a while until things began to work up towards another climax. Mike, as day succeeded day, began to grow accustomed to the life of the bank, and to find that it had its pleasant side after all. Whenever a number of people are working at the same thing, even though that thing is not perhaps what they would have chosen as an object in life, if left to themselves, there is bound to exist an atmosphere of good-fellowship; something akin to, though a hundred times weaker than, the public school spirit. Such a community lacks the main motive of the public school spirit, which is pride in the school and its achievements. Nobody can be proud of the achievements of a bank. When the business of arranging a new Japanese loan was given to the New Asiatic Bank, its employees did not stand on stools, and cheer. On the contrary, they thought of the extra work it would involve; and they cursed a good deal, though there was no denying that it was a big thing for the bank – not unlike winning the Ashburton would be to a school. There is a cold impersonality about a bank. A school is a living thing.

Setting aside this important difference, there was a good deal of the public school about the New Asiatic Bank. The heads of departments were not quite so autocratic as masters, and one was treated more on a grown-up scale, as man to man; but, nevertheless, there remained a distinct flavour of a school republic. Most of the men in the bank, with the exception of certain hard-headed Scotch youths drafted in from other establishments in the City, were old public school men. Mike found two Old Wrykinians in the first week. Neither was well known to him. They had left in his second year in the team. But it was pleasant to have them about, and to feel that they had been educated at the right place.

As far as Mike's personal comfort went, the presence of these two Wrykinians was very much for the good. Both of them knew all about his cricket, and they spread the news. The New Asiatic Bank, like most London banks, was keen on sport, and happened to possess a cricket team which could make a good game with most of the second-rank clubs. The disappearance to the East of two of the best bats of the previous season caused Mike's advent to be hailed with a good deal of enthusiasm. Mike was a county man. He had only played once for his county, it was true, but that did not matter. He had passed the barrier which separates the second-class bat from the first-class, and the bank welcomed him with awe. County men did not come their way every day.

Mike did not like being in the bank, considered in the light of a career. But he bore no grudge against the inmates of the bank, such as he had borne against the inmates of Sedleigh. He had looked on the latter as bound up with the school, and, consequently, enemies. His fellow workers in the bank he regarded as companions in misfortune. They were all in the same boat together. There were men from Tonbridge, Dulwich, Bedford, St Paul's, and a dozen other schools. One or two of them he knew by repute from the pages of Wisden. Bannister, his cheerful predecessor in the Postage Department, was the Bannister, he recollected now, who had played for Geddington against Wrykyn in his second year in the Wrykyn team. Munroe, the big man in the Fixed Deposits, he remembered as leader of the Ripton pack. Every day brought fresh discoveries of this sort, and each made Mike more reconciled to his lot. They were a pleasant set of fellows in the New Asiatic Bank, and but for the dreary outlook which the future held – for Mike, unlike most of his fellow workers, was not attracted by the idea of a life in the East – he would have been very fairly content.

The hostility of Mr Bickersdyke was a slight drawback. Psmith had developed a habit of taking Mike with him to the club of an evening; and this did not do anything towards wiping out of the manager's mind the recollection of his former passage of arms with the Old Wrykinian. The glass remaining Set Fair as far as Mr Rossiter's approval was concerned, Mike was enabled to keep off the managerial carpet to a great extent; but twice, when he posted letters without going through the preliminary formality of stamping them, Mr Bickersdyke had opportunities of which he availed himself. But for these incidents life was fairly enjoyable. Owing to Psmith's benevolent efforts, the Postage Department became quite a happy family, and ex-occupants of the postage desk, Bannister especially, were amazed at the change that had come over Mr Rossiter. He no longer darted from his lair like a pouncing panther. To report his subordinates to the manager seemed now to be a lost art with him. The sight of Psmith and Mr Rossiter proceeding high and disposedly to a mutual lunch became quite common, and ceased to excite remark.

'By kindness,' said Psmith to Mike, after one of these ex-peditions. 'By tact and kindness. That is how it is done. I do not despair of training Comrade Rossiter one of these days to jump through paper hoops.'

So that, altogether, Mike's life in the bank had become very fairly pleasant.

Out of office-hours he enjoyed himself hugely. London was strange to him, and with Psmith as a companion, he extracted a vast deal of entertainment from it. Psmith was not unac-quainted with the West End, and he proved an excellent guide. At first Mike expostulated with unfailing regularity at the other's habit of paying for everything, but Psmith waved aside all objections with languid firmness.

'I need you, Comrade Jackson,' he said, when Mike lodged a protest on finding himself bound for the stalls for the second night in succession. 'We must stick together. As my confidential secretary and adviser, your place is by my side. Who knows but that between the acts tonight I may not be seized with some luminous thought? Could I utter this to my next-door neigh-bour or the programme-girl? Stand by me, Comrade Jackson, or we are undone.'

So Mike stood by him.

By this time Mike had grown so used to his work that he could tell to within five minutes when a rush would come; and he was able to spend a good deal of his time reading a sur-reptitious novel behind a pile of ledgers, or down in the tea-room. The New Asiatic Bank supplied tea to its employees. In quality it was bad, and the bread-and-butter associated with it was worse. But it had the merit of giving one an excuse for being away from one's desk. There were large printed notices all over the tea-room, which was in the basement, informing gentlemen that they were only allowed ten minutes for tea, but one took just as long as one thought the head of one's department would stand, from twenty-five minutes to an hour and a quarter.

This state of things was too good to last. Towards the beginning of the New Year a new man arrived, and Mike was moved on to another department.

14. Mr Waller Appears in a New Light

The department into which Mike was sent was the Cash, or, to be more exact, that section of it which was known as Paying Cashier. The important task of shooting doubloons across the counter did not belong to Mike himself, but to Mr Waller. Mike's work was less ostentatious, and was performed with pen, ink, and ledgers in the background. Occasionally, when Mr Waller was out at lunch, Mike had to act as substitute for him, and cash cheques; but Mr Waller always went out at a slack time, when few customers came in, and Mike seldom had any very startling sum to hand over.

He enjoyed being in the Cash Department. He liked Mr Waller. The work was easy; and when he did happen to make mistakes, they were corrected patiently by the grey-bearded one, and not used as levers for boosting him into the presence of Mr Bickersdyke, as they might have been in some departments. The cashier seemed to have taken a fancy to Mike; and Mike, as was usually the way with him when people went out of their way to be friendly, was at his best. Mike at his ease and unsuspicious of hostile intentions was a different person from Mike with his prickles out.

Psmith, meanwhile, was not enjoying himself. It was an unheard-of thing, he said, depriving a man of his confidential secretary without so much as asking his leave.

'It has caused me the greatest inconvenience,' he told Mike, drifting round in a melancholy way to the Cash Department during a slack spell one afternoon. 'I miss you at every turn. Your keen intelligence and ready sympathy were invaluable to me. Now where am I? In the cart. I evolved a slightly bright thought on life just now. There was nobody to tell it to except the new man. I told it him, and the fool gaped. I tell you, Comrade Jackson, I feel like some lion that has been robbed of its cub. I feel as Marshall would feel if they took Snelgrove away from him, or as Peace might if he awoke one morning to

75

find Plenty gone. Comrade Rossiter does his best. We still talk brokenly about Manchester United – they got routed in the first round of the Cup yesterday and Comrade Rossiter is wearing black – but it is not the same. I try work, but that is no good either. From ledger to ledger they hurry me, to stifle my regret. And when they win a smile from me, they think that I forget. But I don't. I am a broken man. That new exhibit they've got in your place is about as near to the Extreme Edge as anything I've ever seen. One of Nature's blighters. Well, well, I must away. Comrade Rossiter awaits me.'

Mike's successor, a youth of the name of Bristow, was causing Psmith a great deal of pensive melancholy. His worst defect – which he could not help – was that he was not Mike. His others – which he could – were numerous. His clothes were cut in a way that harrowed Psmith's sensitive soul every time he looked at them. The fact that he wore detachable cuffs, which he took off on beginning work and stacked in a glistening pile on the desk in front of him, was no proof of innate viciousness of disposition, but it prejudiced the Old Etonian against him. It was part of Psmith's philosophy that a man who wore detachable cuffs had passed beyond the limit of human toleration. In addition, Bristow wore a small black moustache and a ring and that, as Psmith informed Mike, put the lid on it.

Mike would sometimes stroll round to the Postage Department to listen to the conversations between the two. Bristow was always friendliness itself. He habitually addressed Psmith as Smithy, a fact which entertained Mike greatly but did not seem to amuse Psmith to any overwhelming extent. On the other hand, when, as he generally did, he called Mike 'Mister Cricketer', the humour of the thing appeared to elude Mike, though the mode of address always drew from Psmith a pale, wan smile, as of a broken heart made cheerful against its own inclination.

The net result of the coming of Bristow was that Psmith spent most of his time, when not actually oppressed by a rush of work, in the precincts of the Cash Department, talking to Mike and Mr Waller. The latter did not seem to share the dislike common among the other heads of departments of seeing his subordinates receiving visitors. Unless the work was really heavy, in which case a mild remonstrance escaped him, he offered no objection to Mike being at home to Psmith. It was this tolerance which sometimes got him into trouble with Mr Bickersdyke. The manager did not often perambulate the office, but he did occasionally, and the interview which ensued upon his finding Hutchinson, the underling in the Cash Department at that time, with his stool tilted comfortably against the wall, reading the sporting news from a pink paper to a friend from the Outward Bills Department who lay luxuriously on the floor beside him, did not rank among Mr Waller's pleasantest memories. But Mr Waller was too soft-hearted to interfere with his assistants unless it was absolutely necessary. The truth of the matter was that the New Asiatic Bank was over-staffed. There were too many men for the work. The London branch of the bank was really only a nursery. New men were constantly wanted in the Eastern branches, so they had to be put into the London branch to learn the business, whether there was any work for them to do or not.

It was after one of these visits of Psmith's that Mr Waller displayed a new and unsuspected side to his character. Psmith had come round in a state of some depression to discuss Bristow, as usual. Bristow, it seemed, had come to the bank that morning in a fancy waistcoat of so emphatic a colour-scheme that Psmith stoutly refused to sit in the same department with it.

'What with Comrades Bristow and Bickersdyke combined,' said Psmith plaintively, 'the work is becoming too hard for me. The whisper is beginning to circulate, "Psmith's number is up. As a reformer he is merely among those present. He is losing his dash." But what can I do? I cannot keep an eye on both of them at the same time. The moment I concentrate myself on Comrade Bickersdyke for a brief spell, and seem to be doing him a bit of good, what happens? Why, Comrade Bristow sneaks off and buys a sort of woollen sunset. I saw the thing unexpectedly. I tell you I was shaken. It is the suddenness of that waistcoat which hits you. It's discouraging, this sort of thing. I try always to think well of my fellow man. As an energetic Socialist, I do my best to see the good that is in him, but it's hard. Comrade Bristow's the most striking argument against the equality of man I've ever come across.'

Mr Waller intervened at this point.

'I think you must really let Jackson go on with his work, Smith,' he said. 'There seems to be too much talking.'

'My besetting sin,' said Psmith sadly. 'Well, well, I will go back and do my best to face it, but it's a tough job.'

He tottered wearily away in the direction of the Postage Department.

'Oh, Jackson,' said Mr Waller, 'will you kindly take my place for a few minutes? I must go round and see the Inward Bills about something. I shall be back very soon.'

Mike was becoming accustomed to deputizing for the cashier for short spaces of time. It generally happened that he had to do so once or twice a day. Strictly speaking, perhaps, Mr Waller was wrong to leave such an important task as the actual cashing of cheques to an inexperienced person of Mike's standing; but the New Asiatic Bank differed from most banks in that there was not a great deal of cross-counter work. People came in fairly frequently to cash cheques of two or three pounds, but it was rare that any very large dealings took place.

Having completed his business with the Inward Bills, Mr Waller made his way back by a circuitous route, taking in the Postage desk.

He found Psmith with a pale, set face, inscribing figures in a ledger. The Old Etonian greeted him with the faint smile of a persecuted saint who is determined to be cheerful even at the stake.

'Comrade Bristow,' he said.

'Hullo, Smithy?' said the other, turning.

Psmith sadly directed Mr Waller's attention to the waistcoat, which was certainly definite in its colouring.

'Nothing,' said Psmith. 'I only wanted to look at you.'

'Funny ass,' said Bristow, resuming his work. Psmith glanced at Mr Waller, as who should say, 'See what I have to put up with. And yet I do not give way.'

'Oh – er – Smith,' said Mr Waller, 'when you were talking to Jackson just now – '

'Say no more,' said Psmith. 'It shall not occur again. Why should I dislocate the work of your department in my efforts to win a sympathetic word? I will bear Comrade Bristow like a man here. After all, there are worse things at the Zoo.'

'No, no,' said Mr Waller hastily, 'I did not mean that. By all means pay us a visit now and then, if it does not interfere with your own work. But I noticed just now that you spoke to Bristow as Comrade Bristow.'

'It is too true,' said Psmith. 'I must correct myself of the habit. He will be getting above himself.'

'And when you were speaking to Jackson, you spoke of yourself as a Socialist.'

'Socialism is the passion of my life,' said Psmith.

Mr Waller's face grew animated. He stammered in his eagerness.

'I am delighted,' he said. 'Really, I am delighted. I also – '

'A fellow worker in the Cause?' said Psmith.

'Er – exactly.'

Psmith extended his hand gravely. Mr Waller shook it with enthusiasm.

'I have never liked to speak of it to anybody in the office,' said Mr Waller, 'but I, too, am heart and soul in the movement.'

'Yours for the Revolution?' said Psmith.

'Just so. Just so. Exactly. I was wondering – the fact is, I am in the habit of speaking on Sundays in the open air, and – '

'Hyde Park?'

'No. No. Clapham Common. It is – er – handier for me where I live. Now, as you are interested in the movement, I was thinking that perhaps you might care to come and hear me speak next Sunday. Of course, if you have nothing better to do.'

'I should like to excessively,' said Psmith.

'Excellent. Bring Jackson with you, and both of you come to supper afterwards, if you will.'

'Thanks very much.'

'Perhaps you would speak yourself?'

'No,' said Psmith. 'No. I think not. My Socialism is rather of the practical sort. I seldom speak. But it would be a treat to listen to you. What – er – what type of oratory is yours?'

'Oh, well,' said Mr Waller, pulling nervously at his beard, 'of course I – . Well, I am perhaps a little bitter – '

'Yes, yes.'

'A little mordant and ironical.'

'You would be,' agreed Psmith. 'I shall look forward to Sunday with every fibre quivering. And Comrade Jackson shall be at my side.'

'Excellent,' said Mr Waller. 'I will go and tell him now.'

15. Stirring Times on the Common

'The first thing to do,' said Psmith, 'is to ascertain that such a place as Clapham Common really exists. One has heard of it, of course, but has its existence ever been proved? I think not. Having accomplished that, we must then try to find out how to get to it. I should say at a venture that it would necessitate a sea-voyage. On the other hand, Comrade Waller, who is a native of the spot, seems to find no difficulty in rolling to the office every morning. Therefore – you follow me, Jackson? – it must be in England. In that case, we will take a taximeter cab, and go out into the unknown, hand in hand, trusting to luck.'

'I expect you could get there by tram,' said Mike.

Psmith suppressed a slight shudder.

'I fear, Comrade Jackson,' he said, 'that the old *noblesse oblige* traditions of the Psmiths would not allow me to do that. No. We will stroll gently, after a light lunch, to Trafalgar Square, and hail a taxi.'

'Beastly expensive.'

'But with what an object! Can any expenditure be called excessive which enables us to hear Comrade Waller being mordant and ironical at the other end?'

'It's a rum business,' said Mike. 'I hope the dickens he won't mix us up in it. We should look frightful fools.'

'I may possibly say a few words,' said Psmith carelessly, 'if the spirit moves me. Who am I that I should deny people a simple pleasure?'

Mike looked alarmed.

'Look here,' he said, 'I say, if you *are* going to play the goat, for goodness' sake don't go lugging me into it. I've got heaps of troubles without that.'

Psmith waved the objection aside.

'You,' he said, 'will be one of the large, and, I hope, interested audience. Nothing more. But it is quite possible that the spirit may not move me. I may not feel inspired to speak. I am not one of those who love speaking for speaking's sake. If I have no message for the many-headed, I shall remain silent.'

'Then I hope the dickens you won't have,' said Mike. Of all things he hated most being conspicuous before a crowd – except at cricket, which was a different thing – and he had an uneasy feeling that Psmith would rather like it than otherwise.

'We shall see,' said Psmith absently. 'Of course, if in the vein, I might do something big in the way of oratory. I am a plain, blunt man, but I feel convinced that, given the opportunity, I should haul up my slacks to some effect. But – well, we shall see. We shall see.'

And with this ghastly state of doubt Mike had to be content.

It was with feelings of apprehension that he accompanied Psmith from the flat to Trafalgar Square in search of a cab which should convey them to Clapham Common.

They were to meet Mr Waller at the edge of the Common nearest the old town of Clapham. On the journey down Psmith was inclined to be *débonnaire*. Mike, on the other hand, was silent and apprehensive. He knew enough of Psmith to know that, if half an opportunity were offered him, he would extract entertainment from this affair after his own fashion; and then the odds were that he himself would be dragged into it. Perhaps – his scalp bristled at the mere idea – he would even be let in for a speech.

This grisly thought had hardly come into his head, when Psmith spoke.

'I'm not half sure,' he said thoughtfully, 'I sha'n't call on you for a speech, Comrade Jackson.'

'Look here, Psmith – ' began Mike agitatedly.

'I don't know. I think your solid, incisive style would rather go down with the masses. However, we shall see, we shall see.'

Mike reached the Common in a state of nervous collapse.

Mr Waller was waiting for them by the railings near the pond. The apostle of the Revolution was clad soberly in black, except for a tie of vivid crimson. His eyes shone with the light of enthusiasm, vastly different from the mild glow of amiability which they exhibited for six days in every week. The man was transformed.

'Here you are,' he said. 'Here you are. Excellent. You are in good time. Comrades Wotherspoon and Prebble have already begun to speak. I shall commence now that you have come. This is the way. Over by these trees.'

They made their way towards a small clump of trees, near which a fair-sized crowd had already begun to collect. Evidently listening to the speakers was one of Clapham's fashionable Sunday amusements. Mr Waller talked and gesticulated incessantly as he walked. Psmith's demeanour was perhaps a shade patronizing, but he displayed interest. Mike proceeded to the meeting with the air of an about-to-be-washed dog. He was loathing the whole business with a heartiness worthy of a better cause. Somehow, he felt he was going to be made to look a fool before the afternoon was over. But he registered a vow that nothing should drag him on to the small platform which had been erected for the benefit of the speaker.

As they drew nearer, the voices of Comrades Wotherspoon and Prebble became more audible. They had been audible all the time, very much so, but now they grew in volume. Comrade Wotherspoon was a tall, thin man with side-whiskers and a high voice. He scattered his aitches as a fountain its sprays in a strong wind. He was very earnest. Comrade Prebble was earnest, too. Perhaps even more so than Comrade Wotherspoon. He was handicapped to some extent, however, by not having a palate. This gave to his profoundest thoughts a certain weirdness, as if they had been uttered in an unknown tongue. The crowd was thickest round his platform. The grown-up section plainly regarded him as a comedian, pure and simple, and roared with happy laughter when he urged them to march upon Park Lane and loot the same without mercy or scruple. The children were more doubtful. Several had broken down, and been led away in tears.

When Mr Waller got up to speak on platform number three, his audience consisted at first only of Psmith, Mike, and a fox-terrier. Gradually however, he attracted others. After wavering for a while, the crowd finally decided that he was worth hearing. He had a method of his own. Lacking the natural gifts which marked Comrade Prebble out as an entertainer, he made up for this by his activity. Where his colleagues stood comparatively still, Mr Waller behaved with the vivacity generally supposed to belong only to peas on shovels and cats on hot bricks. He crouched to denounce the House of Lords. He bounded from side to side while dissecting the methods of the plutocrats. During an impassioned onslaught on the monarchical system he stood on one leg and hopped. This was more the sort of thing the crowd had come to see. Comrade Wotherspoon found himself deserted, and even Comrade Prebble's shortcomings in the way of palate were insufficient to keep his flock together. The entire strength of the audience gathered in front of the third platform.

Mike, separated from Psmith by the movement of the crowd, listened with a growing depression. That feeling which attacks a sensitive person sometimes at the theatre when somebody is making himself ridiculous on the stage – the illogical feeling that it is he and not the actor who is floundering – had come over him in a wave. He liked Mr Waller, and it made his gorge rise to see him exposing himself to the jeers of a crowd. The fact that Mr Waller himself did not know that they were jeers, but mistook them for applause, made it no better. Mike felt vaguely furious.

His indignation began to take a more personal shape when the speaker, branching off from the main subject of Socialism, began to touch on temperance. There was no particular reason why Mr Waller should have introduced the subject of temperance, except that he happened to be an enthusiast. He linked it on to his remarks on Socialism by attributing the lethargy of the masses to their fondness for alcohol; and the crowd, which had been inclined rather to pat itself on the back during the assaults on Rank and Property, finding itself assailed in its turn, resented it. They were there to listen to speakers telling them that they were the finest fellows on earth, not pointing out their little failings to them. The feeling of the meeting became hostile. The jeers grew more frequent and less good-tempered.

'Comrade Waller means well,' said a voice in Mike's ear, 'but if he shoots it at them like this much more there'll be a bit of an imbroglio.'

'Look here, Smith,' said Mike quickly, 'can't we stop him? These chaps are getting fed up, and they look bargees enough to do anything. They'll be going for him or something soon.'

'How can we switch off the flow? I don't see. The man is wound up. He means to get it off his chest if it snows. I feel we are by way of being in the soup once more, Comrade Jackson. We can only sit tight and look on.'

The crowd was becoming more threatening every minute. A group of young men of the loafer class who stood near Mike were especially fertile in comment. Psmith's eyes were on the speaker; but Mike was watching this group closely. Suddenly he saw one of them, a thick-set youth wearing a cloth cap and no collar, stoop.

When he rose again there was a stone in his hand.

The sight acted on Mike like a spur. Vague rage against nobody in particular had been simmering in him for half an hour. Now it concentrated itself on the cloth-capped one.

Mr Waller paused momentarily before renewing his harangue. The man in the cloth cap raised his hand. There was a swirl in the crowd, and the first thing that Psmith saw as he turned was Mike seizing the would-be marksman round the neck and hurling him to the ground, after the manner of a forward at football tackling an opponent during a line-out from touch.

There is one thing which will always distract the attention of a crowd from any speaker, and that is a dispute between two of its units. Mr Waller's views on temperance were forgotten in an instant. The audience surged round Mike and his opponent.

The latter had scrambled to his feet now, and was looking round for his assailant.

'That's 'im, Bill!' cried eager voices, indicating Mike.

' 'E's the bloke wot 'it yer, Bill,' said others, more precise in detail.

Bill advanced on Mike in a sidelong, crab-like manner.

' 'Oo're you, I should like to know?' said Bill.

Mike, rightly holding that this was merely a rhetorical question and that Bill had no real thirst for information as to his family history, made no reply. Or, rather, the reply he made was not verbal. He waited till his questioner was within range, and then hit him in the eye. A reply far more satisfactory, if not to Bill himself, at any rate to the interested onlookers, than any flow of words.

A contented sigh went up from the crowd. Their Sunday afternoon was going to be spent just as they considered Sunday afternoons should be spent.

'Give us your coat,' said Psmith briskly, 'and try and get it over quick. Don't go in for any fancy sparring. Switch it on, all you know, from the start. I'll keep a thoughtful eye open to see that none of his friends and relations join in.'

Outwardly Psmith was unruffled, but inwardly he was not feeling so composed. An ordinary turn-up before an impartial crowd which could be relied upon to preserve the etiquette of these matters was one thing. As regards the actual little dispute with the cloth-capped Bill, he felt that he could rely on Mike to handle it satisfactorily. But there was no knowing how long the crowd would be content to remain mere spectators. There was no doubt which way its sympathies lay. Bill, now stripped of his coat and sketching out in a hoarse voice a scenario of what he intended to do – knocking Mike down and stamping him into the mud was one of the milder feats he promised to perform for the entertainment of an indulgent audience – was plainly the popular favourite.

Psmith, though he did not show it, was more than a little apprehensive.

Mike, having more to occupy his mind in the immediate present, was not anxious concerning the future. He had the great advantage over Psmith of having lost his temper. Psmith could look on the situation as a whole, and count the risks and possibilities. Mike could only see Bill shuffling towards him with his head down and shoulders bunched.

'Gow it, Bill!' said someone.

'Pliy up, the Arsenal!' urged a voice on the outskirts of the crowd.

A chorus of encouragement from kind friends in front: 'Step up, Bill!'

And Bill stepped.

16. Further Developments

Bill (surname unknown) was not one of your ultra-scientific fighters. He did not favour the American crouch and the artistic feint. He had a style wholly his own. It seemed to have been modelled partly on a tortoise and partly on a windmill. His head he appeared to be trying to conceal between his shoulders, and he whirled his arms alternately in circular sweeps.

Mike, on the other hand, stood upright and hit straight, with the result that he hurt his knuckles very much on his opponent's skull, without seeming to disturb the latter to any great extent. In the process he received one of the windmill swings on the left ear. The crowd, strong pro-Billites, raised a cheer.

This maddened Mike. He assumed the offensive. Bill, satisfied for the moment with his success, had stepped back, and was indulging in some fancy sparring, when Mike sprang upon him like a panther. They clinched, and Mike, who had got the under grip, hurled Bill forcibly against a stout man who looked like a publican. The two fell in a heap, Bill underneath.

At the same time Bill's friends joined in.

The first intimation Mike had of this was a violent blow across the shoulders with a walking-stick. Even if he had been wearing his overcoat, the blow would have hurt. As he was in his jacket it hurt more than anything he had ever experienced in his life. He leapt up with a yell, but Psmith was there before him. Mike saw his assailant lift the stick again, and then collapse as the old Etonian's right took him under the chin.

He darted to Psmith's side.

'This is no place for us,' observed the latter sadly. 'Shift ho, I think. Come on.'

They dashed simultaneously for the spot where the crowd was thinnest. The ring which had formed round Mike and Bill had broken up as the result of the intervention of Bill's allies, and at the spot for which they ran only two men were standing. And these had apparently made up their minds that neutrality was the best policy, for they made no movement to stop them. Psmith and Mike charged through the gap, and raced for the road.

The suddenness of the move gave them just the start they needed. Mike looked over his shoulder. The crowd, to a man, seemed to be following. Bill, excavated from beneath the publican, led the field. Lying a good second came a band of three, and after them the rest in a bunch.

They reached the road in this order.

Some fifty yards down the road was a stationary tram. In the ordinary course of things it would probably have moved on long before Psmith and Mike could have got to it; but the conductor, a man with sporting blood in him, seeing what appeared to be the finish of some Marathon Race, refrained from giving the signal, and moved out into the road to observe events more clearly, at the same time calling to the driver, who joined him. Passengers on the roof stood up to get a good view. There was some cheering.

Psmith and Mike reached the tram ten yards to the good; and, if it had been ready to start then, all would have been well. But Bill and his friends had arrived while the driver and conductor were both out in the road.

The affair now began to resemble the doings of Horatius on the bridge. Psmith and Mike turned to bay on the platform at the foot of the tram steps. Bill, leading by three yards, sprang on to it, grabbed Mike, and fell with him on to the road. Psmith, descending with a dignity somewhat lessened by the fact that his hat was on the side of his head, was in time to engage the runners-up.

Psmith, as pugilist, lacked something of the calm majesty which characterized him in the more peaceful moments of life, but he was undoubtedly effective. Nature had given him an enormous reach and a lightness on his feet remarkable in one of his size; and at some time in his career he appeared to have learned how to use his hands. The first of the three runners, the walking-stick manipulator, had the misfortune to charge straight into the old Etonian's left. It was a well-timed blow, and the force of it, added to the speed at which the victim was running, sent him on to the pavement, where he spun round and sat down. In the subsequent proceedings he took no part.

The other two attacked Psmith simultaneously, one on each

side. In doing so, the one on the left tripped over Mike and Bill, who were still in the process of sorting themselves out, and fell, leaving Psmith free to attend to the other. He was a tall, weedy youth. His conspicuous features were a long nose and a light yellow waistcoat. Psmith hit him on the former with his left and on the latter with his right. The long youth emitted a gurgle, and collided with Bill, who had wrenched himself free from Mike and staggered to his feet. Bill, having received a second blow in the eye during the course of his interview on the road with Mike, was not feeling himself. Mistaking the other for an enemy, he proceeded to smite him in the parts about the jaw. He had just upset him, when a stern official voice observed, ' 'Ere, now, what's all this?'

There is no more unfailing corrective to a scene of strife than the 'What's all this?' of the London policeman. Bill abandoned his intention of stamping on the prostrate one, and the latter, sitting up, blinked and was silent.

'What's all this?' asked the policeman again. Psmith, adjusting his hat at the correct angle again, undertook the explanations.

'A distressing scene, officer,' he said. 'A case of that unbridled brawling which is, alas, but too common in our London streets. These two, possibly till now the closest friends, fall out over some point, probably of the most trivial nature, and what happens? They brawl. They – '

'He 'it me,' said the long youth, dabbing at his face with a handkerchief and pointing an accusing finger at Psmith, who regarded him through his eyeglass with a look in which pity and censure were nicely blended.

Bill, meanwhile, circling round restlessly, in the apparent hope of getting past the Law and having another encounter with Mike, expressed himself in a stream of language which drew stern reproof from the shocked constable.

'You 'op it,' concluded the man in blue. 'That's what you do. You 'op it.'

'I should,' said Psmith kindly. 'The officer is speaking in your best interests. A man of taste and discernment, he knows what is best. His advice is good, and should be followed.'

The constable seemed to notice Psmith for the first time. He turned and stared at him. Psmith's praise had not had the effect of softening him. His look was one of suspicion.

'And what might *you* have been up to?' he inquired coldly. 'This man says you hit him.'

Psmith waved the matter aside.

'Purely in self-defence,' he said, 'purely in self-defence. What else could the man of spirit do? A mere tap to discourage an aggressive movement.'

The policeman stood silent, weighing matters in the balance. He produced a notebook and sucked his pencil. Then he called the conductor of the tram as a witness.

'A brainy and admirable step,' said Psmith, approvingly. 'This rugged, honest man, all unused to verbal subtleties, shall give us his plain account of what happened. After which, as I presume this tram – little as I know of the habits of trams – has got to go somewhere today, I would suggest that we all separated and moved on.'

He took two half-crowns from his pocket, and began to clink them meditatively together. A slight softening of the frigidity of the constable's manner became noticeable. There was a milder beam in the eyes which gazed into Psmith's.

Nor did the conductor seem altogether uninfluenced by the sight.

The conductor deposed that he had bin on the point of pushing on, seeing as how he'd hung abart long enough, when he see'd them two gents, the long 'un with the heye-glass (Psmith bowed) and t'other 'un, a-legging of it dahn the road towards him, with the other blokes pelting after 'em. He added that, when they reached the trem, the two gents had got aboard, and was then set upon by the blokes. And after that, he concluded, well, there was a bit of a scrap, and that's how it was.

'Lucidly and excellently put,' said Psmith. 'That is just how it was. Comrade Jackson, I fancy we leave the court without a stain on our characters. We win through. Er – constable, we have given you a great deal of trouble. Possibly – ?'

'Thank you, sir.' There was a musical clinking. 'Now then, all of you, you 'op it. You're all bin poking your noses in 'ere long enough. Pop off. Get on with that tram, conductor.'

Psmith and Mike settled themselves in a seat on the roof. When the conductor came along, Psmith gave him half a crown, and asked after his wife and the little ones at home. The conductor thanked goodness that he was a bachelor, punched the tickets, and retired.

'Subject for a historical picture,' said Psmith. 'Wounded leaving the field after the Battle of Clapham Common. How are your injuries, Comrade Jackson?'

'My back's hurting like blazes,' said Mike. 'And my ear's all sore where that chap got me. Anything the matter with you?'

'Physically,' said Psmith, 'no. Spiritually much. Do you realize, Comrade Jackson, the thing that has happened? I am riding in a tram. I, Psmith, have paid a penny for a ticket on a tram. If this should get about the clubs! I tell you, Comrade Jackson, no such crisis has ever occurred before in the course of my career.'

'You can always get off, you know,' said Mike.

'He thinks of everything,' said Psmith, admiringly. 'You have touched the spot with an unerring finger. Let us descend. I observe in the distance a cab. That looks to me more the sort of thing we want. Let us go and parley with the driver.'

17. Sunday Supper

The cab took them back to the flat, at considerable expense, and Psmith requested Mike to make tea, a performance in which he himself was interested purely as a spectator. He had views on the subject of tea-making which he liked to expound from an armchair or sofa, but he never got further than this. Mike, his back throbbing dully from the blow he had received, and feeling more than a little sore all over, prepared the Etna, fetched the milk, and finally produced the finished article.

Psmith sipped meditatively.

'How pleasant,' he said, 'after strife is rest. We shouldn't have appreciated this simple cup of tea had our sensibilities remained unstirred this afternoon. We can now sit at our ease, like warriors after the fray, till the time comes for setting out to Comrade Waller's once more.'

Mike looked up.

'What! You don't mean to say you're going to sweat out to Clapham again?'

'Undoubtedly. Comrade Waller is expecting us to supper.'

'What absolute rot! We can't fag back there.'

'Noblesse oblige. The cry has gone round the Waller household, "Jackson and Psmith are coming to supper," and we cannot disappoint them now. Already the fatted blanc-mange has been killed, and the table creaks beneath what's left of the midday beef. We must be there; besides, don't you want to see how the poor man is? Probably we shall find him in the act of emitting his last breath. I expect he was lynched by the enthusiastic mob.'

'Not much,' grinned Mike. 'They were too busy with us. All right, I'll come if you really want me to, but it's awful rot.'

One of the many things Mike could never understand in Psmith was his fondness for getting into atmospheres that were not his own. He would go out of his way to do this. Mike, like most boys of his age, was never really happy and at his ease except in the presence of those of his own years and class, Psmith, on the contrary, seemed to be bored by them, and infinitely preferred talking to somebody who lived in quite another world. Mike was not a snob. He simply had not the ability to be at his ease with people in another class from his own. He did not know what to talk to them about, unless they were cricket professionals. With them he was never at a loss.

But Psmith was different. He could get on with anyone. He seemed to have the gift of entering into their minds and seeing things from their point of view.

As regarded Mr Waller, Mike liked him personally, and was prepared, as we have seen, to undertake considerable risks in his defence; but he loathed with all his heart and soul the idea of supper at his house. He knew that he would have nothing to say. Whereas Psmith gave him the impression of looking forward to the thing as a treat.

The house where Mr Waller lived was one of a row of semi-detached villas on the north side of the Common. The door was opened to them by their host himself. So far from looking battered and emitting last breaths, he appeared particularly spruce. He had just returned from Church, and was still wearing his gloves and tall hat. He squeaked with surprise when he saw who were standing on the mat.

'Why, dear me, dear me,' he said. 'Here you are! I have been wondering what had happened to you. I was afraid that you might have been seriously hurt. I was afraid those ruffians might have injured you. When last I saw you, you were being – '

'Chivvied,' interposed Psmith, with dignified melancholy. 'Do not let us try to wrap the fact up in pleasant words. We were being chivvied. We were legging it with the infuriated mob at our heels. An ignominious position for a Shropshire Psmith, but, after all, Napoleon did the same.'

'But what happened? I could not see. I only know that quite suddenly the people seemed to stop listening to me, and all gathered round you and Jackson. And then I saw that Jackson was engaged in a fight with a young man.'

'Comrade Jackson, I imagine, having heard a great deal about all men being equal, was anxious to test the theory, and see whether Comrade Bill was as good a man as he was. The

92

experiment was broken off prematurely, but I personally should be inclined to say that Comrade Jackson had a shade the better of the exchanges.'

Mr Waller looked with interest at Mike, who shuffled and felt awkward. He was hoping that Psmith would say nothing about the reason of his engaging Bill in combat. He had an uneasy feeling that Mr Waller's gratitude would be effusive and overpowering, and he did not wish to pose as the brave young hero. There are moments when one does not feel equal to the *rôle*.

Fortunately, before Mr Waller had time to ask any further questions, the supper-bell sounded, and they went into the dining-room.

Sunday supper, unless done on a large and informal scale, is probably the most depressing meal in existence. There is a chill discomfort in the round of beef, an icy severity about the open jam tart. The blancmange shivers miserably.

Spirituous liquor helps to counteract the influence of these things, and so does exhilarating conversation. Unfortunately, at Mr Waller's table there was neither. The cashier's views on temperance were not merely for the platform; they extended to the home. And the company was not of the exhilarating sort. Besides Psmith and Mike and their host, there were four people present – Comrade Prebble, the orator; a young man of the name of Richards; Mr Waller's niece, answering to the name of Ada, who was engaged to Mr Richards; and Edward.

Edward was Mr Waller's son. He was ten years old, wore a very tight Eton suit, and had the peculiarly loathsome expression which a snub nose sometimes gives to the young.

It would have been plain to the most casual observer that Mr Waller was fond and proud of his son. The cashier was a widower, and after five minutes' acquaintance with Edward, Mike felt strongly that Mrs Waller was the lucky one. Edward sat next to Mike, and showed a tendency to concentrate his conversation on him. Psmith, at the opposite end of the table, beamed in a fatherly manner upon the pair through his eyeglass.

Mike got on with small girls reasonably well. He preferred them at a distance, but, if cornered by them, could put up a fairly good show. Small boys, however, filled him with a sort of frozen horror. It was his view that a boy should not be exhibited publicly until he reached an age when he might be in the running for some sort of colours at a public school.

Edward was one of those well-informed small boys. He opened on Mike with the first mouthful.

'Do you know the principal exports of Marseilles?' he inquired.

'What?' said Mike coldly.

'Do you know the principal exports of Marseilles? I do.'

'Oh?' said Mike.

'Yes. Do you know the capital of Madagascar?'

Mike, as crimson as the beef he was attacking, said he did not.

'I do.'

'Oh?' said Mike.

'Who was the first king – '

'You mustn't worry Mr Jackson, Teddy,' said Mr Waller, with a touch of pride in his voice, as who should say 'There are not many boys of his age, I can tell you, who *could* worry you with questions like that.'

'No, no, he likes it,' said Psmith, unnecessarily. 'He likes it. I always hold that much may be learned by casual chit-chat across the dinner-table. I owe much of my own grasp of – '

'I bet *you* don't know what's the capital of Madagascar,' interrupted Mike rudely.

'I do,' said Edward. 'I can tell you the kings of Israel?' he added, turning to Mike. He seemed to have no curiosity as to the extent of Psmith's knowledge. Mike's appeared to fascinate him.

Mike helped himself to beetroot in moody silence.

His mouth was full when Comrade Prebble asked him a question. Comrade Prebble, as has been pointed out in an earlier part of the narrative, was a good chap, but had no roof to his mouth.

'I beg your pardon?' said Mike.

Comrade Prebble repeated his observation. Mike looked helplessly at Psmith, but Psmith's eyes were on his plate.

Mike felt he must venture on some answer.

'No,' he said decidedly.

Comrade Prebble seemed slightly taken aback. There was an awkward pause. Then Mr Waller, for whom his fellow Socialist's methods of conversation held no mysteries, interpreted.

'The mustard, Prebble? Yes, yes. Would you mind passing Prebble the mustard, Mr Jackson?'

'Oh, sorry,' gasped Mike, and, reaching out, upset the water-jug into the open jam-tart.

Through the black mist which rose before his eyes as he leaped to his feet and stammered apologies came the dispassionate voice of Master Edward Waller reminding him that mustard was first introduced into Peru by Cortez.

His host was all courtesy and consideration. He passed the matter off genially. But life can never be quite the same after you have upset a water-jug into an open jam-tart at the table of a comparative stranger. Mike's nerve had gone. He ate on, but he was a broken man.

At the other end of the table it became gradually apparent that things were not going on altogether as they should have done. There was a sort of bleakness in the atmosphere. Young Mr Richards was looking like a stuffed fish, and the face of Mr Waller's niece was cold and set.

'Why, come, come, Ada,' said Mr Waller, breezily, 'what's the matter? You're eating nothing. What's George been saying to you?' he added jocularly.

'Thank you, uncle Robert,' replied Ada precisely, 'there's nothing the matter. Nothing that Mr Richards can say to me can upset me.'

'Mr Richards!' echoed Mr Waller in astonishment. How was he to know that, during the walk back from church, the world had been transformed, George had become Mr Richards, and all was over?

'I assure you, Ada –' began that unfortunate young man. Ada turned a frigid shoulder towards him.

'Come, come,' said Mr Waller disturbed. 'What's all this? What's all this?'

His niece burst into tears and left the room.

If there is anything more embarrassing to a guest than a family row, we have yet to hear of it. Mike, scarlet to the extreme edges of his ears, concentrated himself on his plate. Comrade Prebble made a great many remarks, which were probably illuminating, if they could have been understood. Mr Waller looked, astonished, at Mr Richards. Mr Richards, pink but dogged, loosened his collar, but said nothing. Psmith, leaning forward, asked Master Edward Waller his opinion on the Licensing Bill.

'We happened to have a word or two,' said Mr Richards at length, 'on the way home from church on the subject of Women's Suffrage.'

'That fatal topic!' murmured Psmith.

'In Australia – ' began Master Edward Waller.

'I was rayther – well, rayther facetious about it,' continued Mr Richards.

Psmith clicked his tongue sympathetically.

'In Australia – ' said Edward.

'I went talking on, laughing and joking, when all of a sudden she flew out at me. How was I to know she was 'eart and soul in the movement? You never told me,' he added accusingly to his host.

'In Australia – ' said Edward.

'I'll go and try and get her round. How was I to know?'

Mr Richards thrust back his chair and bounded from the room.

'Now, iawinyaw, iear oller – ' said Comrade Prebble judicially, but was interrupted.

'How very disturbing!' said Mr Waller. 'I am so sorry that this should have happened. Ada is such a touchy, sensitive girl. She – '

'In Australia,' said Edward in even tones, 'they've *got* Women's Suffrage already. Did *you* know that?' he said to Mike.

Mike made no answer. His eyes were fixed on his plate. A bead of perspiration began to roll down his forehead. If his feelings could have been ascertained at that moment, they would have been summed up in the words, 'Death, where is thy sting?'

18. Psmith Makes a Discovery

'Women,' said Psmith, helping himself to trifle, and speaking with the air of one launched upon his special subject, 'are, one must recollect, like – like – er, well, in fact, just so. Passing on lightly from that conclusion, let us turn for a moment to the Rights of Property, in connection with which Comrade Prebble and yourself had so much that was interesting to say this afternoon. Perhaps you' – he bowed in Comrade Prebble's direction – 'would resume, for the benefit of Comrade Jackson – a novice in the Cause, but earnest – your very lucid – '

Comrade Prebble beamed, and took the floor. Mike began to realize that, till now, he had never known what boredom meant. There had been moments in his life which had been less interesting than other moments, but nothing to touch this for agony. Comrade Prebble's address streamed on like water rushing over a weir. Every now and then there was a word or two which was recognizable, but this happened so rarely that it amounted to little. Sometimes Mr Waller would interject a remark, but not often. He seemed to be of the opinion that Comrade Prebble's was the master mind and that to add anything to his views would be in the nature of painting the lily and gilding the refined gold. Mike himself said nothing. Psmith and Edward were equally silent. The former sat like one in a trance, thinking his own thoughts, while Edward, who, prospecting on the sideboard, had located a rich biscuit-mine, was too occupied for speech.

After about twenty minutes, during which Mike's discomfort changed to a dull resignation, Mr Waller suggested a move to the drawing-room, where Ada, he said, would play some hymns.

The prospect did not dazzle Mike, but any change, he thought, must be for the better. He had sat staring at the ruin of the blancmange so long that it had begun to hypnotize him. Also, the move had the excellent result of eliminating the snub-nosed Edward, who was sent to bed. His last words were in the form of a question, addressed to Mike, on the subject of the hypotenuse and the square upon the same.

'A remarkably intelligent boy,' said Psmith. 'You must let him come to tea at our flat one day. I may not be in myself – I have many duties which keep me away – but Comrade Jackson is sure to be there, and will be delighted to chat with him.'

On the way upstairs Mike tried to get Psmith to himself for a moment to suggest the advisability of an early departure; but Psmith was in close conversation with his host. Mike was left to Comrade Prebble, who, apparently, had only touched the fringe of his subject in his lecture in the dining-room.

When Mr Waller had predicted hymns in the drawing-room, he had been too sanguine (or too pessimistic). Of Ada, when they arrived, there were no signs. It seemed that she had gone straight to bed. Young Mr Richards was sitting on the sofa, moodily turning the leaves of a photograph album, which contained portraits of Master Edward Waller in geometrically progressing degrees of repulsiveness – here, in frocks, looking like a gargoyle; there, in sailor suit, looking like nothing on earth. The inspection of these was obviously deepening Mr Richards' gloom, but he proceeded doggedly with it.

Comrade Prebble backed the reluctant Mike into a corner, and, like the Ancient Mariner, held him with a glittering eye. Psmith and Mr Waller, in the opposite corner, were looking at something with their heads close together. Mike definitely abandoned all hope of a rescue from Psmith, and tried to buoy himself up with the reflection that this could not last for ever.

Hours seemed to pass, and then at last he heard Psmith's voice saying good-bye to his host.

He sprang to his feet. Comrade Prebble was in the middle of a sentence, but this was no time for polished courtesy. He felt that he must get away, and at once. 'I fear,' Psmith was saying, 'that we must tear ourselves away. We have greatly enjoyed our evening. You must look us up at our flat one day, and bring Comrade Prebble. If I am not in, Comrade Jackson is certain to be, and he will be more than delighted to hear Comrade Prebble speak further on the subject of which he is such a master.' Comrade Prebble was understood to say that he would certainly come. Mr Waller beamed. Mr Richards, still steeped in gloom, shook hands in silence.

Out in the road, with the front door shut behind them, Mike spoke his mind.

'Look here, Smith,' he said definitely, 'if being your confidential secretary and adviser is going to let me in for any more of that sort of thing, you can jolly well accept my resignation.'

'The orgy was not to your taste?' said Psmith sympathetically.

Mike laughed. One of those short, hollow, bitter laughs.

'I am at a loss, Comrade Jackson,' said Psmith, 'to understand your attitude. You fed sumptuously. You had fun with the crockery – that knockabout act of yours with the water-jug was alone worth the money – and you had the advantage of listening to the views of a master of his subject. What more do you want?'

'What on earth did you land me with that man Prebble for?'

'Land you! Why, you courted his society. I had practically to drag you away from him. When I got up to say good-bye, you were listening to him with bulging eyes. I never saw such a picture of rapt attention. Do you mean to tell me, Comrade Jackson, that your appearance belied you, that you were not interested? Well, well. How we misread our fellow creatures.'

'I think you might have come and lent a hand with Prebble. It was a bit thick.'

'I was too absorbed with Comrade Waller. We were talking of things of vital moment. However, the night is yet young. We will take this cab, wend our way to the West, seek a café, and cheer ourselves with light refreshments.'

Arrived at a café whose window appeared to be a sort of museum of every kind of German sausage, they took possession of a vacant table and ordered coffee. Mike soon found himself soothed by his bright surroundings, and gradually his impressions of blancmange, Edward, and Comrade Prebble faded from his mind. Psmith, meanwhile, was preserving an unusual silence, being deep in a large square book of the sort in which Press cuttings are pasted. As Psmith scanned its contents a curious smile lit up his face. His reflections seemed to be of an agreeable nature.

'Hullo,' said Mike, 'what have you got hold of there? Where did you get that?'

'Comrade Waller very kindly lent it to me. He showed it to me after supper, knowing how enthusiastically I was attached to the Cause. Had you been less tensely wrapped up in Comrade Prebble's conversation, I would have desired you to step across and join us. However, you now have your opportunity.'

'But what is it?' asked Mike.

'It is the record of the meetings of the Tulse Hill Parliament,' said Psmith impressively. 'A faithful record of all they said, all the votes of confidence they passed in the Government, and also all the nasty knocks they gave it from time to time.'

'What on earth's the Tulse Hill Parliament?'

'It is, alas,' said Psmith in a grave, sad voice, 'no more. In life it was beautiful, but now it has done the Tom Bowling act. It has gone aloft. We are dealing, Comrade Jackson, not with the live, vivid present, but with the far-off, rusty past. And yet, in a way, there is a touch of the live, vivid present mixed up in it.'

'I don't know what the dickens you're talking about,' said Mike. 'Let's have a look, anyway.'

Psmith handed him the volume, and, leaning back, sipped his coffee, and watched him. At first Mike's face was bored and blank, but suddenly an interested look came into it.

'Aha!' said Psmith.

'Who's Bickersdyke? Anything to do with our Bickersdyke?'

'No other than our genial friend himself.'

Mike turned the pages, reading a line or two on each.

'Hullo!' he said, chuckling. 'He lets himself go a bit, doesn't he!'

'He does,' acknowledged Psmith. 'A fiery, passionate nature, that of Comrade Bickersdyke.'

'He's simply cursing the Government here. Giving them frightful beans.'

Psmith nodded.

'I noticed the fact myself.'

'But what's it all about?'

'As far as I can glean from Comrade Waller,' said Psmith, 'about twenty years ago, when he and Comrade Bickersdyke worked hand-in-hand as fellow clerks at the New Asiatic, they were both members of the Tulse Hill Parliament, that powerful institution. At that time Comrade Bickersdyke was as fruity a Socialist as Comrade Waller is now. Only, apparently, as he

100

began to get on a bit in the world, he altered his views to some extent as regards the iniquity of freezing on to a decent share of the doubloons. And that, you see, is where the dim and rusty past begins to get mixed up with the live, vivid present. If any tactless person were to publish those very able speeches made by Comrade Bickersdyke when a bulwark of the Tulse Hill Parliament, our revered chief would be more or less caught bending, if I may employ the expression, as regards his chances of getting in as Unionist candidate at Kenningford. You follow me, Watson? I rather fancy the light-hearted electors of Kenningford, from what I have seen of their rather acute sense of humour, would be, as it were, all over it. It would be very, very trying for Comrade Bickersdyke if these speeches of his were to get about.'

'You aren't going to – !'

'I shall do nothing rashly. I shall merely place this handsome volume among my treasured books. I shall add it to my "Books that have helped me" series. Because I fancy that, in an emergency, it may not be at all a bad thing to have about me. And now,' he concluded, 'as the hour is getting late, perhaps we had better be shoving off for home.'

19. The Illness of Edward

Life in a bank is at its pleasantest in the winter. When all the world outside is dark and damp and cold, the light and warmth of the place are comforting. There is a pleasant air of solidity about the interior of a bank. The green shaded lamps look cosy. And, the outside world offering so few attractions, the worker, perched on his stool, feels that he is not so badly off after all. It is when the days are long and the sun beats hot on the pavement, and everything shouts to him how splendid it is out in the country, that he begins to grow restless.

Mike, except for a fortnight at the beginning of his career in the New Asiatic Bank, had not had to stand the test of sunshine. At present, the weather being cold and dismal, he was almost entirely contented. Now that he had got into the swing of his work, the days passed very quickly; and with his life after office-hours he had no fault to find at all.

His life was very regular. He would arrive in the morning just in time to sign his name in the attendance-book before it was removed to the accountant's room. That was at ten o'clock. From ten to eleven he would potter. There was nothing going on at that time in his department, and Mr Waller seemed to take it for granted that he should stroll off to the Postage Department and talk to Psmith, who had generally some fresh grievance against the ring-wearing Bristow to air. From eleven to half past twelve he would put in a little gentle work. Lunch, unless there was a rush of business or Mr Waller happened to suffer from a spasm of conscientiousness, could be spun out from half past twelve to two. More work from two till half past three. From half past three till half past four tea in the tea-room, with a novel. And from half past four till five either a little more work or more pottering, according to whether there was any work to do or not. It was by no means an unpleasant mode of spending a late January day.

Then there was no doubt that it was an interesting little community, that of the New Asiatic Bank. The curiously amateurish nature of the institution lent a certain air of lightheartedness to the place. It was not like one of those banks whose London office is their main office, where stern business is everything and a man becomes a mere machine for getting through a certain amount of routine work. The employees of the New Asiatic Bank, having plenty of time on their hands, were able to retain their individuality. They had leisure to think of other things besides their work. Indeed, they had so much leisure that it is a wonder they thought of their work at all.

The place was full of quaint characters. There was West, who had been requested to leave Haileybury owing to his habit of borrowing horses and attending meets in the neighbourhood, the same being always out of bounds and necessitating a complete disregard of the rules respecting evening chapel and lock-up. He was a small, dried-up youth, with black hair plastered down on his head. He went about his duties in a costume which suggested the sportsman of the comic papers.

There was also Hignett, who added to the meagre salary allowed him by the bank by singing comic songs at the minor music halls. He confided to Mike his intention of leaving the bank as soon as he had made a name, and taking seriously to the business. He told him that he had knocked them at the Bedford the week before, and in support of the statement showed him a cutting from the *Era*, in which the writer said that 'Other acceptable turns were the Bounding Zouaves, Steingruber's Dogs, and Arthur Hignett.' Mike wished him luck.

And there was Raymond who dabbled in journalism and was the author of 'Straight Talks to Housewives' in *Trifles,* under the pseudonym of 'Lady Gussie'; Wragge, who believed that the earth was flat, and addressed meetings on the subject in Hyde Park on Sundays; and many others, all interesting to talk to of a morning when work was slack and time had to be filled in.

Mike found himself, by degrees, growing quite attached to the New Asiatic Bank.

One morning, early in February, he noticed a curious change in Mr Waller. The head of the Cash Department was, as a rule, mildly cheerful on arrival, and apt (excessively, Mike thought, though he always listened with polite interest) to relate the most recent sayings and doings of his snub-nosed son, Edward. No action of this young prodigy was withheld from Mike. He had heard, on different occasions, how he had won a prize at his school for General Information (which Mike could well believe); how he had trapped young Mr Richards, now happily reconciled to Ada, with an ingenious verbal catch; and how he had made a sequence of diverting puns on the name of the new curate, during the course of that cleric's first Sunday afternoon visit.

On this particular day, however, the cashier was silent and absent-minded. He answered Mike's good-morning mechanically, and sitting down at his desk, stared blankly across the building. There was a curiously grey, tired look on his face.

Mike could not make it out. He did not like to ask if there was anything the matter. Mr Waller's face had the unreasonable effect on him of making him feel shy and awkward. Anything in the nature of sorrow always dried Mike up and robbed him of the power of speech. Being naturally sympathetic, he had raged inwardly in many a crisis at this devil of dumb awkwardness which possessed him and prevented him from putting his sympathy into words. He had always envied the cooing readiness of the hero on the stage when anyone was in trouble. He wondered whether he would ever acquire that knack of pouring out a limpid stream of soothing words on such occasions. At present he could get no farther than a scowl and an almost offensive gruffness.

The happy thought struck him of consulting Psmith. It was his hour for pottering, so he pottered round to the Postage Department, where he found the old Etonian eyeing with disfavour a new satin tie which Bristow was wearing that morning for the first time.

'I say, Smith,' he said, 'I want to speak to you for a second.'

Psmith rose. Mike led the way to a quiet corner of the Telegrams Department.

'I tell you, Comrade Jackson,' said Psmith, 'I am hard pressed. The fight is beginning to be too much for me. After a grim struggle, after days of unremitting toil, I succeeded yesterday in inducing the man Bristow to abandon that rainbow waistcoat of his. Today I enter the building, blythe and buoyant, worn, of course, from the long struggle, but seeing with aching eyes the dawn of another, better era, and there is Comrade Bristow in a satin tie. It's hard, Comrade Jackson, it's hard, I tell you.'

'Look here, Smith,' said Mike, 'I wish you'd go round to the Cash and find out what's up with old Waller. He's got the hump about something. He's sitting there looking absolutely fed up with things. I hope there's nothing up. He's not a bad sort. It would be rot if anything rotten's happened.'

Psmith began to display a gentle interest.

'So other people have troubles as well as myself,' he murmured musingly. 'I had almost forgotten that. Comrade Waller's misfortunes cannot but be trivial compared with mine, but possibly it will be as well to ascertain their nature. I will reel round and make inquiries.'

'Good man,' said Mike. 'I'll wait here.'

Psmith departed, and returned, ten minutes later, looking more serious than when he had left.

'His kid's ill, poor chap,' he said briefly. 'Pretty badly too, from what I can gather. Pneumonia. Waller was up all night. He oughtn't to be here at all today. He doesn't know what he's doing half the time. He's absolutely fagged out. Look here, you'd better nip back and do as much of the work as you can. I shouldn't talk to him much if I were you. Buck along.'

Mike went. Mr Waller was still sitting staring out across the aisle. There was something more than a little gruesome in the sight of him. He wore a crushed, beaten look, as if all the life and fight had gone out of him. A customer came to the desk to cash a cheque. The cashier shovelled the money to him under the bars with the air of one whose mind is elsewhere. Mike could guess what he was feeling, and what he was thinking about. The fact that the snub-nosed Edward was, without exception, the most repulsive small boy he had ever met in this world, where repulsive small boys crowd and jostle one another, did not interfere with his appreciation of the cashier's state of mind. Mike's was essentially a sympathetic character. He had the gift of intuitive understanding, where people of whom he was fond were concerned. It was this which drew to him those who had intelligence enough to see beyond his sometimes rather forbidding manner, and to realize that his blunt speech was largely due to shyness. In spite of his prejudice against Edward, he could put himself into Mr Waller's place, and see the thing from his point of view.

Psmith's injunction to him not to talk much was unnecessary. Mike, as always, was rendered utterly dumb by the sight of suffering. He sat at his desk, occupying himself as best he could with the driblets of work which came to him.

Mr Waller's silence and absentness continued unchanged. The habit of years had made his work mechanical. Probably few of the customers who came to cash cheques suspected that there was anything the matter with the man who paid them their money. After all, most people look on the cashier of a bank as a sort of human slot-machine. You put in your cheque, and out comes money. It is no affair of yours whether life is treating the machine well or ill that day.

The hours dragged slowly by till five o'clock struck, and the cashier, putting on his coat and hat, passed silently out through the swing-doors. He walked listlessly. He was evidently tired out.

Mike shut his ledger with a vicious bang, and went across to find Psmith. He was glad the day was over.

20. Concerning a Cheque

Things never happen quite as one expects them to. Mike came to the office next morning prepared for a repetition of the previous day. He was amazed to find the cashier not merely cheerful, but even exuberantly cheerful. Edward, it appeared, had rallied in the afternoon, and, when his father had got home, had been out of danger. He was now going along excellently, and had stumped Ada, who was nursing him, with a question about the Thirty Years' War, only a few minutes before his father had left to catch his train. The cashier was overflowing with happiness and goodwill towards his species. He greeted customers with bright remarks on the weather, and snappy views on the leading events of the day: the former tinged with optimism, the latter full of a gentle spirit of toleration. His attitude towards the latest actions of His Majesty's Government was that of one who felt that, after all, there was probably some good even in the vilest of his fellow creatures, if one could only find it.

Altogether, the cloud had lifted from the Cash Department. All was joy, jollity, and song.

'The attitude of Comrade Waller,' said Psmith, on being informed of the change, 'is reassuring. I may now think of my own troubles. Comrade Bristow has blown into the office today in patent leather boots with white kid uppers, as I believe the technical term is. Add to that the fact that he is still wearing the satin tie, the waistcoat, and the ring, and you will understand why I have definitely decided this morning to abandon all hope of his reform. Henceforth my services, for what they are worth, are at the disposal of Comrade Bickersdyke. My time from now onward is his. He shall have the full educative value of my exclusive attention. I give Comrade Bristow up. Made straight for the corner flag, you understand,' he added, as Mr Rossiter emerged from his lair, 'and centred, and Sandy Turnbull headed a beautiful goal. I was just telling Jackson about the match against Blackburn Rovers,' he said to Mr Rossiter.

'Just so, just so. But get on with your work, Smith. We are a little behind-hand. I think perhaps it would be as well not to leave it just yet.'

'I will leap at it at once,' said Psmith cordially.

Mike went back to his department.

The day passed quickly. Mr Waller, in the intervals of work, talked a good deal, mostly of Edward, his doings, his sayings, and his prospects. The only thing that seemed to worry Mr Waller was the problem of how to employ his son's almost superhuman talents to the best advantage. Most of the goals towards which the average man strives struck him as too unambitious for the prodigy.

By the end of the day Mike had had enough of Edward. He never wished to hear the name again.

We do not claim originality for the statement that things never happen quite as one expects them to. We repeat it now because of its profound truth. The Edward's pneumonia episode having ended satisfactorily (or, rather, being apparently certain to end satisfactorily, for the invalid, though out of danger, was still in bed), Mike looked forward to a series of days unbroken by any but the minor troubles of life. For these he was prepared. What he did not expect was any big calamity.

At the beginning of the day there were no signs of it. The sky was blue and free from all suggestions of approaching thunderbolts. Mr Waller, still chirpy, had nothing but good news of Edward. Mike went for his morning stroll round the office feeling that things had settled down and had made up their mind to run smoothly.

When he got back, barely half an hour later, the storm had burst.

There was no one in the department at the moment of his arrival; but a few minutes later he saw Mr Waller come out of the manager's room, and make his way down the aisle.

It was his walk which first gave any hint that something was wrong. It was the same limp, crushed walk which Mike had seen when Edward's safety still hung in the balance.

As Mr Waller came nearer, Mike saw that the cashier's face was deadly pale.

Mr Waller caught sight of him and quickened his pace.

'Jackson,' he said.

Mike came forward.

'Do you – remember – ' he spoke slowly, and with an effort, 'do you remember a cheque coming through the day before yesterday for a hundred pounds, with Sir John Morrison's signature?'

'Yes. It came in the morning, rather late.'

Mike remembered the cheque perfectly well, owing to the amount. It was the only three-figure cheque which had come across the counter during the day. It had been presented just before the cashier had gone out to lunch. He recollected the man who had presented it, a tallish man with a beard. He had noticed him particularly because of the contrast between his manner and that of the cashier. The former had been so very cheery and breezy, the latter so dazed and silent.

'Why,' he said.

'It was a forgery,' muttered Mr Waller, sitting down heavily.

Mike could not take it in all at once. He was stunned. All he could understand was that a far worse thing had happened than anything he could have imagined.

'A forgery?' he said.

'A forgery. And a clumsy one. Oh it's hard. I should have seen it on any other day but that. I could not have missed it. They showed me the cheque in there just now. I could not believe that I had passed it. I don't remember doing it. My mind was far away. I don't remember the cheque or anything about it. Yet there it is.'

Once more Mike was tongue-tied. For the life of him he could not think of anything to say. Surely, he thought, he could find *something* in the shape of words to show his sympathy. But he could find nothing that would not sound horribly stilted and cold. He sat silent.

'Sir John is in there,' went on the cashier. 'He is furious. Mr Bickersdyke, too. They are both furious. I shall be dismissed. I shall lose my place. I shall be dismissed.' He was talking more to himself than to Mike. It was dreadful to see him sitting there, all limp and broken.

'I shall lose my place. Mr Bickersdyke has wanted to get rid of me for a long time. He never liked me. I shall be dismissed. What can I do? I'm an old man. I can't make another start. I am good for nothing. Nobody will take an old man like me.'

His voice died away. There was a silence. Mike sat staring miserably in front of him.

Then, quite suddenly, an idea came to him. The whole pressure of the atmosphere seemed to lift. He saw a way out. It was a curious crooked way, but at that moment it stretched clear and broad before him. He felt lighthearted and excited, as if he were watching the development of some interesting play at the theatre.

He got up, smiling.

The cashier did not notice the movement. Somebody had come in to cash a cheque, and he was working mechanically.

Mike walked up the aisle to Mr Bickersdyke's room, and went in.

The manager was in his chair at the big table. Opposite him, facing slightly sideways, was a small, round, very red-faced man. Mr Bickersdyke was speaking as Mike entered.

'I can assure you, Sir John – ' he was saying.

He looked up as the door opened.

'Well, Mr Jackson?'

Mike almost laughed. The situation was tickling him.

'Mr Waller has told me – ' he began.

'I have already seen Mr Waller.'

'I know. He told me about the cheque. I came to explain.'

'Explain?'

'Yes. He didn't cash it at all.'

'I don't understand you, Mr Jackson.'

'I was at the counter when it was brought in,' said Mike. 'I cashed it.'

21. Psmith Makes Inquiries

Psmith, as was his habit of a morning when the fierce rush of his commercial duties had abated somewhat, was leaning gracefully against his desk, musing on many things, when he was aware that Bristow was standing before him.

Focusing his attention with some reluctance upon this blot on the horizon, he discovered that the exploiter of rainbow waistcoats and satin ties was addressing him.

'I say, Smithy,' said Bristow. He spoke in rather an awed voice.

'Say on, Comrade Bristow,' said Psmith graciously. 'You have our ear. You would seem to have something on your chest in addition to that Neapolitan ice garment which, I regret to see, you still flaunt. If it is one tithe as painful as that, you have my sympathy. Jerk it out, Comrade Bristow.'

'Jackson isn't half copping it from old Bick.'

'Isn't – ? What exactly did you say?'

'He's getting it hot on the carpet.'

'You wish to indicate,' said Psmith, 'that there is some slight disturbance, some passing breeze between Comrades Jackson and Bickersdyke?'

Bristow chuckled.

'Breeze! Blooming hurricane, more like it. I was in Bick's room just now with a letter to sign, and I tell you, the fur was flying all over the bally shop. There was old Bick cursing for all he was worth, and a little red-faced buffer puffing out his cheeks in an armchair.'

'We all have our hobbies,' said Psmith.

'Jackson wasn't saying much. He jolly well hadn't a chance. Old Bick was shooting it out fourteen to the dozen.'

'I have been privileged,' said Psmith, 'to hear Comrade Bickersdyke speak both in his sanctum and in public. He has, as you suggest, a ready flow of speech. What, exactly was the cause of the turmoil?'

'I couldn't wait to hear. I was too jolly glad to get away. Old Bick looked at me as if he could eat me, snatched the letter out of my hand, signed it, and waved his hand at the door as a hint to hop it. Which I jolly well did. He had started jawing Jackson again before I was out of the room.'

'While applauding his hustle,' said Psmith, 'I fear that I must take official notice of this. Comrade Jackson is essentially a Sensitive Plant, highly strung, neurotic. I cannot have his nervous system jolted and disorganized in this manner, and his value as a confidential secretary and adviser impaired, even though it be only temporarily. I must look into this. I will go and see if the orgy is concluded. I will hear what Comrade Jackson has to say on the matter. I shall not act rashly, Comrade Bristow. If the man Bickersdyke is proved to have had good grounds for his outbreak, he shall escape uncensured. I may even look in on him and throw him a word of praise. But if I find, as I suspect, that he has wronged Comrade Jackson, I shall be forced to speak sharply to him.'

Mike had left the scene of battle by the time Psmith reached the Cash Department, and was sitting at his desk in a somewhat dazed condition, trying to clear his mind sufficiently to enable him to see exactly how matters stood as concerned himself. He felt confused and rattled. He had known, when he went to the manager's room to make his statement, that there would be trouble. But, then, trouble is such an elastic word. It embraces a hundred degrees of meaning. Mike had expected sentence of dismissal, and he had got it. So far he had nothing to complain of. But he had not expected it to come to him riding high on the crest of a great, frothing wave of verbal denunciation. Mr Bickersdyke, through constantly speaking in public, had developed the habit of fluent denunciation to a remarkable extent. He had thundered at Mike as if Mike had been his Majesty's Government or the Encroaching Alien, or something of that sort. And that kind of thing is a little overwhelming at short range. Mike's head was still spinning.

It continued to spin; but he never lost sight of the fact round which it revolved, namely, that he had been dismissed from the service of the bank. And for the first time he began to wonder what they would say about this at home.

Up till now the matter had seemed entirely a personal one,

He had charged in to rescue the harassed cashier in precisely the same way as that in which he had dashed in to save him from Bill, the Stone-Flinging Scourge of Clapham Common. Mike's was one of those direct, honest minds which are apt to concentrate themselves on the crisis of the moment, and to leave the consequences out of the question entirely.

What would they say at home? That was the point.

Again, what could he do by way of earning a living? He did not know much about the City and its ways, but he knew enough to understand that summary dismissal from a bank is not the best recommendation one can put forward in applying for another job. And if he did not get another job in the City, what could he do? If it were only summer, he might get taken on somewhere as a cricket professional. Cricket was his line. He could earn his pay at that. But it was very far from being summer.

He had turned the problem over in his mind till his head ached, and had eaten in the process one-third of a wooden penholder, when Psmith arrived.

'It has reached me,' said Psmith, 'that you and Comrade Bickersdyke have been seen doing the Hackenschmidt-Gotch act on the floor. When my informant left, he tells me, Comrade B. had got a half-Nelson on you, and was biting pieces out of your ear. Is this so?'

Mike got up. Psmith was the man, he felt, to advise him in this crisis. Psmith's was the mind to grapple with his Hard Case.

'Look here, Smith,' he said, 'I want to speak to you. I'm in a bit of a hole, and perhaps you can tell me what to do. Let's go out and have a cup of coffee, shall we? I can't tell you about it here.'

'An admirable suggestion,' said Psmith. 'Things in the Postage Department are tolerably quiescent at present. Naturally I shall be missed, if I go out. But my absence will not spell irretrievable ruin, as it would at a period of greater commercial activity. Comrades Rossiter and Bristow have studied my methods. They know how I like things to be done. They are fully competent to conduct the business of the department in my absence. Let us, as you say, scud forth. We will go to a Mecca. Why so-called I do not know, nor, indeed, do I ever hope to know. There we may obtain, at a price, a passable cup of coffee, and you shall tell me your painful story.'

The Mecca, except for the curious aroma which pervades all Meccas, was deserted. Psmith, moving a box of dominoes on to the next table, sat down.

'Dominoes,' he said, 'is one of the few manly sports which have never had great attractions for me. A cousin of mine, who secured his chess blue at Oxford, would, they tell me, have represented his University in the dominoes match also, had he not unfortunately dislocated the radius bone of his bazooka while training for it. Except for him, there has been little dominoes talent in the Psmith family. Let us merely talk. What of this slight brass-rag-parting to which I alluded just now? Tell me all.'

He listened gravely while Mike related the incidents which had led up to his confession and the results of the same. At the conclusion of the narrative he sipped his coffee in silence for a moment.

'This habit of taking on to your shoulders the harvest of other people's bloomers,' he said meditatively, 'is growing upon you, Comrade Jackson. You must check it. It is like dram-drinking. You begin in a small way by breaking school rules to extract Comrade Jellicoe (perhaps the supremest of all the blitherers I have ever met) from a hole. If you had stopped there, all might have been well. But the thing, once started, fascinated you. Now you have landed yourself with a splash in the very centre of the Oxo in order to do a good turn to Comrade Waller. You must drop it, Comrade Jackson. When you were free and without ties, it did not so much matter. But now that you are confidential secretary and adviser to a Shropshire Psmith, the thing must stop. Your secretarial duties must be paramount. Nothing must be allowed to interfere with them. Yes. The thing must stop before it goes too far.'

'It seems to me,' said Mike, 'that it has gone too far. I've got the sack. I don't know how much farther you want it to go.'

Psmith stirred his coffee before replying.

'True,' he said, 'things look perhaps a shade rocky just now, but all is not yet lost. You must recollect that Comrade Bickersdyke spoke in the heat of the moment. That generous temperament was stirred to its depths. He did not pick his words. But calm will succeed storm, and we may be able to do something yet. I have some little influence with Comrade Bickersdyke. Wrongly, perhaps,' added Psmith modestly, 'he thinks somewhat highly of my judgement. If he sees that I am opposed to this step, he may possibly reconsider it. What Psmith thinks today, is his motto, I shall think tomorrow. However, we shall see.'

'I bet we shall!' said Mike ruefully.

'There is, moreover,' continued Psmith, 'another aspect to the affair. When you were being put through it, in Comrade Bickersdyke's inimitably breezy manner, Sir John What's-his-name was, I am given to understand, present. Naturally, to pacify the aggrieved bart., Comrade B. had to lay it on regardless of expense. In America, as possibly you are aware, there is a regular post of mistake-clerk, whose duty it is to receive in the neck anything that happens to be coming along when customers make complaints. He is hauled into the presence of the foaming customer, cursed, and sacked. The customer goes away appeased. The mistake-clerk, if the harangue has been unusually energetic, applies for a rise of salary. Now, possibly, in your case – '

'In my case,' interrupted Mike, 'there was none of that rot. Bickersdyke wasn't putting it on. He meant every word. Why, dash it all, you know yourself he'd be only too glad to sack me, just to get some of his own back with me.'

Psmith's eyes opened in pained surprise.

'Get some of his own back!' he repeated.

'Are you insinuating, Comrade Jackson, that my relations with Comrade Bickersdyke are not of the most pleasant and agreeable nature possible? How do these ideas get about? I yield to nobody in my respect for our manager. I may have had occasion from time to time to correct him in some trifling matter, but surely he is not the man to let such a thing rankle? No! I prefer to think that Comrade Bickersdyke regards me as his friend and well-wisher, and will lend a courteous ear to any proposal I see fit to make. I hope shortly to be able to prove this to you. I will discuss this little affair of the cheque with him at our ease at the club, and I shall be surprised if we do not come to some arrangement.'

'Look here, Smith,' said Mike earnestly, 'for goodness' sake don't go playing the goat. There's no earthly need for you to get lugged into this business. Don't you worry about me. I shall be all right.'

'I think,' said Psmith, 'that you will – when I have chatted with Comrade Bickersdyke.'

22. And Takes Steps

On returning to the bank, Mike found Mr Waller in the grip of a peculiarly varied set of mixed feelings. Shortly after Mike's departure for the Mecca, the cashier had been summoned once more into the Presence, and had there been informed that, as apparently he had not been directly responsible for the gross piece of carelessness by which the bank had suffered so considerable a loss (here Sir John puffed out his cheeks like a meditative toad), the matter, as far as he was concerned, was at an end. On the other hand – ! Here Mr Waller was hauled over the coals for Incredible Rashness in allowing a mere junior subordinate to handle important tasks like the paying out of money, and so on, till he felt raw all over. However, it was not dismissal. That was the great thing. And his principal sensation was one of relief.

Mingled with the relief were sympathy for Mike, gratitude to him for having given himself up so promptly, and a curiously dazed sensation, as if somebody had been hitting him on the head with a bolster.

All of which emotions, taken simultaneously, had the effect of rendering him completely dumb when he saw Mike. He felt that he did not know what to say to him. And as Mike, for his part, simply wanted to be let alone, and not compelled to talk, conversation was at something of a standstill in the Cash Department.

After five minutes, it occurred to Mr Waller that perhaps the best plan would be to interview Psmith. Psmith would know exactly how matters stood. He could not ask Mike point-blank whether he had been dismissed. But there was the probability that Psmith had been informed and would pass on the information.

Psmith received the cashier with a dignified kindliness.

'Oh, er, Smith,' said Mr Waller, 'I wanted just to ask you about Jackson.'

Psmith bowed his head gravely.

'Exactly,' he said. 'Comrade Jackson. I think I may say that you have come to the right man. Comrade Jackson has placed himself in my hands, and I am dealing with his case. A somewhat tricky business, but I shall see him through.'

'Has he – ?' Mr Waller hesitated.

'You were saying?' said Psmith.

'Does Mr Bickersdyke intend to dismiss him?'

'At present,' admitted Psmith, 'there is some idea of that description floating – nebulously, as it were – in Comrade Bickersdyke's mind. Indeed, from what I gather from my client, the push was actually administered, in so many words. But tush! And possibly bah! we know what happens on these occasions, do we not? You and I are students of human nature, and we know that a man of Comrade Bickersdyke's warm-hearted type is apt to say in the heat of the moment a great deal more than he really means. Men of his impulsive character cannot help expressing themselves in times of stress with a certain generous strength which those who do not understand them are inclined to take a little too seriously. I shall have a chat with Comrade Bickersdyke at the conclusion of the day's work, and I have no doubt that we shall both laugh heartily over this little episode.'

Mr Waller pulled at his beard, with an expression on his face that seemed to suggest that he was not quite so confident on this point. He was about to put his doubts into words when Mr Rossiter appeared, and Psmith, murmuring something about duty, turned again to his ledger. The cashier drifted back to his own department.

It was one of Psmith's theories of Life, which he was accustomed to propound to Mike in the small hours of the morning with his feet on the mantelpiece, that the secret of success lay in taking advantage of one's occasional slices of luck, in seizing, as it were, the happy moment. When Mike, who had had the passage to write out ten times at Wrykyn on one occasion as an imposition, reminded him that Shakespeare had once said something about there being a tide in the affairs of men, which, taken at the flood, &c., Psmith had acknowledged with an easy grace that possibly Shakespeare *had* got on to it first, and that it was but one more proof of how often great minds thought alike.

Though waiving his claim to the copyright of the maxim, he nevertheless had a high opinion of it, and frequently acted upon it in the conduct of his own life.

Thus, when approaching the Senior Conservative Club at five o'clock with the idea of finding Mr Bickersdyke there, he observed his quarry entering the Turkish Baths which stand some twenty yards from the club's front door, he acted on his maxim, and decided, instead of waiting for the manager to finish his bath before approaching him on the subject of Mike, to corner him in the Baths themselves.

He gave Mr Bickersdyke five minutes' start. Then, reckoning that by that time he would probably have settled down, he pushed open the door and went in himself. And, having paid his money, and left his boots with the boy at the threshold, he was rewarded by the sight of the manager emerging from a box at the far end of the room, clad in the mottled towels which the bather, irrespective of his personal taste in dress, is obliged to wear in a Turkish bath.

Psmith made for the same box. Mr Bickersdyke's clothes lay at the head of one of the sofas, but nobody else had staked out a claim. Psmith took possession of the sofa next to the manager's. Then, humming lightly, he undressed, and made his way downstairs to the Hot Rooms. He rather fancied himself in towels. There was something about them which seemed to suit his figure. They gave him, he though, rather a *débonnaire* look. He paused for a moment before the looking-glass to examine himself, with approval, then pushed open the door of the Hot Rooms and went in.

23. Mr Bickersdyke Makes a Concession

Mr Bickersdyke was reclining in an easy-chair in the first room, staring before him in the boiled-fish manner customary in a Turkish Bath. Psmith dropped into the next seat with a cheery 'Good evening.' The manager started as if some firm hand had driven a bradawl into him. He looked at Psmith with what was intended to be a dignified stare. But dignity is hard to achieve in a couple of parti-coloured towels. The stare did not differ to any great extent from the conventional boiled-fish look, alluded to above.

Psmith settled himself comfortably in his chair. 'Fancy finding you here,' he said pleasantly. 'We seem always to be meeting. To me,' he added, with a reassuring smile, 'it is a great pleasure. A very great pleasure indeed. We see too little of each other during office hours. Not that one must grumble at that. Work before everything. You have your duties, I mine. It is merely unfortunate that those duties are not such as to enable us to toil side by side, encouraging each other with word and gesture. However, it is idle to repine. We must make the most of these chance meetings when the work of the day is over.'

Mr Bickersdyke heaved himself up from his chair and took another at the opposite end of the room. Psmith joined him.

'There's something pleasantly mysterious, to my mind,' said he chattily, 'in a Turkish Bath. It seems to take one out of the hurry and bustle of the everyday world. It is a quiet backwater in the rushing river of Life. I like to sit and think in a Turkish Bath. Except, of course, when I have a congenial companion to talk to. As now. To me – '

Mr Bickersdyke rose, and went into the next room.

'To me,' continued Psmith, again following, and seating himself beside the manager, 'there is, too, something eerie in these places. There is a certain sinister air about the attendants. They glide rather than walk. They say little. Who knows what they may be planning and plotting? That drip-drip again. It may be merely water, but how are we to know that it is not blood? It would be so easy to do away with a man in a Turkish Bath. Nobody has seen him come in. Nobody can trace him if he disappears. These are uncomfortable thoughts, Mr Bickersdyke.'

Mr Bickersdyke seemed to think them so. He rose again, and returned to the first room.

'I have made you restless,' said Psmith, in a voice of self-reproach, when he had settled himself once more by the manager's side. 'I am sorry. I will not pursue the subject. Indeed, I believe that my fears are unnecessary. Statistics show, I understand, that large numbers of men emerge in safety every year from Turkish Baths. There was another matter of which I wished to speak to you. It is a somewhat delicate matter, and I am only encouraged to mention it to you by the fact that you are so close a friend of my father's.'

Mr Bickersdyke had picked up an early edition of an evening paper, left on the table at his side by a previous bather, and was to all appearances engrossed in it. Psmith, however, not discouraged, proceeded to touch upon the matter of Mike.

'There was,' he said, 'some little friction, I hear, in the office today in connection with a cheque.' The evening paper hid the manager's expressive face, but from the fact that the hands holding it tightened their grip Psmith deduced that Mr Bickersdyke's attention was not wholly concentrated on the City news. Moreover, his toes wriggled. And when a man's toes wriggle, he is interested in what you are saying.

'All these petty breezes,' continued Psmith sympathetically, 'must be very trying to a man in your position, a man who wishes to be left alone in order to devote his entire thought to the niceties of the higher Finance. It is as if Napoleon, while planning out some intricate scheme of campaign, were to be called upon in the midst of his meditations to bully a private for not cleaning his buttons. Naturally, you were annoyed. Your giant brain, wrenched temporarily from its proper groove, expended its force in one tremendous reprimand of Comrade Jackson. It was as if one had diverted some terrific electric current which should have been controlling a vast system of machinery, and turned it on to annihilate a black-beetle. In the present case, of course, the result is as might have been expected. Comrade Jackson, not realizing the position of affairs, went away with the absurd idea that all was over, that you meant all you said – briefly, that his number was up. I assured him that he was mistaken, but no! He persisted in declaring that all was over, that you had dismissed him from the bank.'

Mr Bickersdyke lowered the paper and glared bulbously at the old Etonian.

'Mr Jackson is perfectly right,' he snapped. 'Of course I dismissed him.'

'Yes, yes,' said Psmith, 'I have no doubt that at the moment you did work the rapid push. What I am endeavouring to point out is that Comrade Jackson is under the impression that the edict is permanent, that he can hope for no reprieve.'

'Nor can he.'

'You don't mean – '

'I mean what I say.'

'Ah, I quite understand,' said Psmith, as one who sees that he must make allowances. 'The incident is too recent. The storm has not yet had time to expend itself. You have not had leisure to think the matter over coolly. It is hard, of course, to be cool in a Turkish Bath. Your ganglions are still vibrating. Later, perhaps – '

'Once and for all,' growled Mr Bickersdyke, 'the thing is ended. Mr Jackson will leave the bank at the end of the month. We have no room for fools in the office.'

'You surprise me,' said Psmith. 'I should not have thought that the standard of intelligence in the bank was extremely high. With the exception of our two selves, I think that there are hardly any men of real intelligence on the staff. And comrade Jackson is improving every day. Being, as he is, under my constant supervision he is rapidly developing a stranglehold on his duties, which – '

'I have no wish to discuss the matter any further.'

'No, no. Quite so, quite so. Not another word. I am dumb.'

'There are limits you see, to the uses of impertinence, Mr Smith.'

Psmith started.

'You are not suggesting – ! You do not mean that I – !'

'I have no more to say. I shall be glad if you will allow me to read my paper.'

Psmith waved a damp hand.

'I should be the last man,' he said stiffly, 'to force my

conversation on another. I was under the impression that you enjoyed these little chats as keenly as I did. If I was wrong – '

He relapsed into a wounded silence. Mr Bickersdyke resumed his perusal of the evening paper, and presently, laying it down, rose and made his way to the room where muscular attendants were in waiting to perform that blend of Jiu-Jitsu and Catch-as-catch-can which is the most valuable and at the same time most painful part of a Turkish Bath.

It was not till he was resting on his sofa, swathed from head to foot in a sheet and smoking a cigarette, that he realized that Psmith was sharing his compartment.

He made the unpleasant discovery just as he had finished his first cigarette and lighted his second. He was blowing out the match when Psmith, accompanied by an attendant, appeared in the doorway, and proceeded to occupy the next sofa to himself. All that feeling of dreamy peace, which is the reward one receives for allowing oneself to be melted like wax and kneaded like bread, left him instantly. He felt hot and annoyed. To escape was out of the question. Once one has been scientifically wrapped up by the attendant and placed on one's sofa, one is a fixture. He lay scowling at the ceiling, resolved to combat all attempt at conversation with a stony silence.

Psmith, however, did not seem to desire conversation. He lay on his sofa motionless for a quarter of an hour, then reached out for a large book which lay on the table, and began to read.

When he did speak, he seemed to be speaking to himself. Every now and then he would murmur a few words, sometimes a single name. In spite of himself, Mr Bickersdyke found himself listening.

At first the murmurs conveyed nothing to him. Then suddenly a name caught his ear. Strowther was the name, and somehow it suggested something to him. He could not say precisely what. It seemed to touch some chord of memory. He knew no one of the name of Strowther. He was sure of that. And yet it was curiously familiar. An unusual name, too. He could not help feeling that at one time he must have known it quite well.

'Mr Strowther,' murmured Psmith, 'said that the hon. gentleman's remarks would have been nothing short of treason, if they had not been so obviously the mere babblings of an irresponsible lunatic. Cries of "Order, order," and a voice, "Sit down, fat-head!" '

For just one moment Mr Bickersdyke's memory poised motionless, like a hawk about to swoop. Then it darted at the mark. Everything came to him in a flash. The hands of the clock whizzed back. He was no longer Mr John Bickersdyke, manager of the London branch of the New Asiatic Bank, lying on a sofa in the Cumberland Street Turkish Baths. He was Jack Bickersdyke, clerk in the employ of Messrs Norton and Biggleswade, standing on a chair and shouting 'Order! order!' in the Masonic Room of the 'Red Lion' at Tulse Hill, while the members of the Tulse Hill Parliament, divided into two camps, yelled at one another, and young Tom Barlow, in his official capacity as Mister Speaker, waved his arms dumbly, and banged the table with his mallet in his efforts to restore calm.

He remembered the whole affair as if it had happened yesterday. It had been a speech of his own which had called forth the above expression of opinion from Strowther. He remembered Strowther now, a pale, spectacled clerk in Baxter and Abrahams, an inveterate upholder of the throne, the House of Lords and all constituted authority. Strowther had objected to the socialistic sentiments of his speech in connection with the Budget, and there had been a disturbance unparalleled even in the Tulse Hill Parliament, where disturbances were frequent and loud....

Psmith looked across at him with a bright smile. 'They report you verbatim,' he said. 'And rightly. A more able speech I have seldom read. I like the bit where you call the Royal Family "blood-suckers". Even then, it seems you knew how to express yourself fluently and well.'

Mr Bickersdyke sat up. The hands of the clock had moved again, and he was back in what Psmith had called the live, vivid present.

'What have you got there?' he demanded.

'It is a record,' said Psmith, 'of the meeting of an institution called the Tulse Hill Parliament. A bright, chatty little institution, too, if one may judge by these reports. You in particular, if I may say so, appear to have let yourself go with refreshing vim. Your political views have changed a great deal since those days, have they not? It is extremely interesting. A most fascinating study for political students. When I send these speeches of yours to the *Clarion* – '

Mr Bickersdyke bounded on his sofa.

'What!' he cried.

'I was saying,' said Psmith, 'that the *Clarion* will probably make a most interesting comparison between these speeches and those you have been making at Kenningford.'

'I – I – I forbid you to make any mention of these speeches.'

Psmith hesitated.

'It would be great fun seeing what the papers said,' he protested.

'Great fun!'

'It is true,' mused Psmith, 'that in a measure, it would dish you at the election. From what I saw of those light-hearted lads at Kenningford the other night, I should say they would be so amused that they would only just have enough strength left to stagger to the poll and vote for your opponent.'

Mr Bickersdyke broke out into a cold perspiration.

'I forbid you to send those speeches to the papers,' he cried.

Psmith reflected.

'You see,' he said at last, 'it is like this. The departure of Comrade Jackson, my confidential secretary and adviser, is certain to plunge me into a state of the deepest gloom. The only way I can see at present by which I can ensure even a momentary lightening of the inky cloud is the sending of these speeches to some bright paper like the *Clarion*. I feel certain that their comments would wring, at any rate, a sad, sweet smile from me. Possibly even a hearty laugh. I must, therefore, look on these very able speeches of yours in something of the light of an antidote. They will stand between me and black depression. Without them I am in the cart. With them I may possibly buoy myself up.'

Mr Bickersdyke shifted uneasily on his sofa. He glared at the floor. Then he eyed the ceiling as if it were a personal enemy of his. Finally he looked at Psmith. Psmith's eyes were closed in peaceful meditation.

'Very well,' said he at last. 'Jackson shall stop.'

Psmith came out of his thoughts with a start. 'You were observing – ?' he said.

'I shall not dismiss Jackson,' said Mr Bickersdyke.

Psmith smiled winningly.

'Just as I had hoped,' he said. 'Your very justifiable anger melts before reflection. The storm subsides, and you are at leisure to examine the matter dispassionately. Doubts begin to creep in. Possibly, you say to yourself, I have been too hasty, too harsh. Justice must be tempered with mercy. I have caught Comrade Jackson bending, you add (still to yourself), but shall I press home my advantage too ruthlessly? No, you cry, I will abstain. And I applaud your action. I like to see this spirit of gentle toleration. It is bracing and comforting. As for these excellent speeches,' he added, 'I shall, of course, no longer have any need of their consolation. I can lay them aside. The sunlight can now enter and illumine my life through more ordinary channels. The cry goes round, "Psmith is himself again." '

Mr Bickersdyke said nothing. Unless a snort of fury may be counted as anything.

24. The Spirit of Unrest

During the following fortnight, two things happened which materially altered Mike's position in the bank.

The first was that Mr Bickersdyke was elected a member of Parliament. He got in by a small majority amidst scenes of disorder of a nature unusual even in Kenningford. Psmith, who went down on the polling-day to inspect the revels and came back with his hat smashed in, reported that, as far as he could see, the electors of Kenningford seemed to be in just that state of happy intoxication which might make them vote for Mr Bickersdyke by mistake. Also it had been discovered, on the eve of the poll, that the bank manager's opponent, in his youth, had been educated at a school in Germany, and had subsequently spent two years at Heidelberg University. These damaging revelations were having a marked effect on the warm-hearted patriots of Kenningford, who were now referring to the candidate in thick but earnest tones as 'the German Spy'.

'So that taking everything into consideration,' said Psmith, summing up, 'I fancy that Comrade Bickersdyke is home.'

And the papers next day proved that he was right.

'A hundred and fifty-seven,' said Psmith, as he read his paper at breakfast. 'Not what one would call a slashing victory. It is fortunate for Comrade Bickersdyke, I think, that I did not send those very able speeches of his to the *Clarion*.'

Till now Mike had been completely at a loss to understand why the manager had sent for him on the morning following the scene about the cheque, and informed him that he had reconsidered his decision to dismiss him. Mike could not help feeling that there was more in the matter than met the eye. Mr Bickersdyke had not spoken as if it gave him any pleasure to reprieve him. On the contrary, his manner was distinctly brusque. Mike was thoroughly puzzled. To Psmith's statement, that he had talked the matter over quietly with the manager and brought things to a satisfactory conclusion, he had paid little attention. But now he began to see light.

'Great Scott, Smith,' he said, 'did you tell him you'd send those speeches to the papers if he sacked me?'

Psmith looked at him through his eye-glass, and helped himself to another piece of toast.

'I am unable,' he said, 'to recall at this moment the exact terms of the very pleasant conversation I had with Comrade Bickersdyke on the occasion of our chance meeting in the Turkish Bath that afternoon; but, thinking things over quietly now that I have more leisure, I cannot help feeling that he may possibly have read some such intention into my words. You know how it is in these little chats, Comrade Jackson. One leaps to conclusions. Some casual word I happened to drop may have given him the idea you mention. At this distance of time it is impossible to say with any certainty. Suffice it that all has ended well. He *did* reconsider his resolve. I shall be only too happy if it turns out that the seed of the alteration in his views was sown by some careless word of mine. Perhaps we shall never know.'

Mike was beginning to mumble some awkward words of thanks, when Psmith resumed his discourse.

'Be that as it may, however,' he said, 'we cannot but perceive that Comrade Bickersdyke's election has altered our position to some extent. As you have pointed out, he may have been influenced in this recent affair by some chance remark of mine about those speeches. Now, however, they will cease to be of any value. Now that he is elected he has nothing to lose by their publication. I mention this by way of indicating that it is possible that, if another painful episode occurs, he may be more ruthless.'

'I see what you mean,' said Mike. 'If he catches me on the hop again, he'll simply go ahead and sack me.'

'That,' said Psmith, '*is* more or less the position of affairs.'

The other event which altered Mike's life in the bank was his removal from Mr Waller's department to the Fixed Deposits. The work in the Fixed Deposits was less pleasant, and Mr Gregory, the head of the department was not of Mr Waller's type. Mr Gregory, before joining the home-staff of the New Asiatic Bank, had spent a number of years with a firm in the Far East, where he had acquired a liver and a habit of addressing those under him in a way that suggested the mate of a tramp steamer. Even on the days when his liver was not troubling him, he was truculent. And when, as usually happened, it did trouble him, he was a perfect fountain of abuse. Mike and he hated each other from the first. The work in the Fixed Deposits was not really difficult, when you got the hang of it, but there was a certain amount of confusion in it to a beginner; and Mike, in commercial matters, was as raw a beginner as ever began. In the two other departments through which he had passed, he had done tolerably well. As regarded his work in the Postage Department, stamping letters and taking them down to the post office was just about his form. It was the sort of work on which he could really get a grip. And in the Cash Department, Mr Waller's mild patience had helped him through. But with Mr Gregory it was different. Mike hated being shouted at. It confused him. And Mr Gregory invariably shouted. He always spoke as if he were competing against a high wind. With Mike he shouted more than usual. On his side, it must be admitted that Mike was something out of the common run of bank clerks. The whole system of banking was a horrid mystery to him. He did not understand why things were done, or how the various departments depended on and dove-tailed into one another. Each department seemed to him something separate and distinct. Why they were all in the same building at all he never really gathered. He knew that it could not be purely from motives of sociability, in order that the clerks might have each other's company during slack spells. That much he suspected, but beyond that he was vague.

It naturally followed that, after having grown, little by little, under Mr Waller's easy-going rule, to enjoy life in the bank, he now suffered a reaction. Within a day of his arrival in the Fixed Deposits he was loathing the place as earnestly as he had loathed it on the first morning.

Psmith, who had taken his place in the Cash Department, reported that Mr Waller was inconsolable at his loss.

'I do my best to cheer him up,' he said, 'and he smiles bravely every now and then. But when he thinks I am not looking, his head droops and that wistful expression comes into his face. The sunshine has gone out of his life.'

It had just come into Mike's, and, more than anything else, was making him restless and discontented. That is to say, it was now late spring: the sun shone cheerfully on the City; and cricket was in the air. And that was the trouble.

In the dark days, when everything was fog and slush, Mike had been contented enough to spend his mornings and afternoons in the bank, and go about with Psmith at night. Under such conditions, London is the best place in which to be, and the warmth and light of the bank were pleasant.

But now things had changed. The place had become a prison. With all the energy of one who had been born and bred in the country, Mike hated having to stay indoors on days when all the air was full of approaching summer. There were mornings when it was almost more than he could do to push open the swing doors, and go out of the fresh air into the stuffy atmosphere of the bank.

The days passed slowly, and the cricket season began. Instead of being a relief, this made matters worse. The little cricket he could get only made him want more. It was as if a starving man had been given a handful of wafer biscuits.

If the summer had been wet, he might have been less restless. But, as it happened, it was unusually fine. After a week of cold weather at the beginning of May, a hot spell set in. May passed in a blaze of sunshine. Large scores were made all over the country.

Mike's name had been down for the M.C.C. for some years, and he had become a member during his last season at Wrykyn. Once or twice a week he managed to get up to Lord's for half an hour's practice at the nets; and on Saturdays the bank had matches, in which he generally managed to knock the cover off rather ordinary club bowling. But it was not enough for him.

June came, and with it more sunshine. The atmosphere of the bank seemed more oppressive than ever.

25. At the Telephone

If one looks closely into those actions which are apparently due
to sudden impulse, one generally finds that the sudden impulse
was merely the last of a long series of events which led up to the
action. Alone, it would not have been powerful enough to effect
anything. But, coming after the way has been paved for it, it is
irresistible. The hooligan who bonnets a policeman is apparently the victim of a sudden impulse. In reality, however, the
bonneting is due to weeks of daily encounters with the constable, at each of which meetings the dislike for his helmet and
the idea of smashing it in grow a little larger, till finally they
blossom into the deed itself.

This was what happened in Mike's case. Day by day, through
the summer, as the City grew hotter and stuffier, his hatred of
the bank became more and more the thought that occupied his
mind. It only needed a moderately strong temptation to make
him break out and take the consequences.

Psmith noticed his restlessness and endeavoured to soothe
it.

'All is not well,' he said, 'with Comrade Jackson, the Sunshine of the Home. I note a certain wanness of the cheek. The
peach-bloom of your complexion is no longer up to sample.
Your eye is wild; your merry laugh no longer rings through the
bank, causing nervous customers to leap into the air with
startled exclamations. You have the manner of one whose only
friend on earth is a yellow dog, and who has lost the dog. Why
is this, Comrade Jackson?'

They were talking in the flat at Clement's Inn. The night was
hot. Through the open windows the roar of the Strand sounded
faintly. Mike walked to the window and looked out.

'I'm sick of all this rot,' he said shortly.

Psmith shot an inquiring glance at him, but said nothing. This
restlessness of Mike's was causing him a good deal of inconvenience, which he bore in patient silence, hoping for better

times. With Mike obviously discontented and out of tune with all the world, there was but little amusement to be extracted from the evenings now. Mike did his best to be cheerful, but he could not shake off the caged feeling which made him restless.

'What rot it all is!' went on Mike, sitting down again. 'What's the good of it all? You go and sweat all day at a desk, day after day, for about twopence a year. And when you're about eighty-five, you retire. It isn't living at all. It's simply being a bally vegetable.'

'You aren't hankering, by any chance, to be a pirate of the Spanish main, or anything like that, are you?' inquired Psmith.

'And all this rot about going out East,' continued Mike. 'What's the good of going out East?'

'I gather from casual chit-chat in the office that one becomes something of a blood when one goes out East,' said Psmith. 'Have a dozen native clerks under you, all looking up to you as the Last Word in magnificence, and end by marrying the Governor's daughter.'

'End by getting some foul sort of fever, more likely, and being booted out as no further use to the bank.'

'You look on the gloomy side, Comrade Jackson. I seem to see you sitting in an armchair, fanned by devoted coolies, telling some Eastern potentate that you can give him five minutes. I understand that being in a bank in the Far East is one of the world's softest jobs. Millions of natives hang on your lightest word. Enthusiastic rajahs draw you aside and press jewels into your hand as a token of respect and esteem. When on an elephant's back you pass, somebody beats on a booming brass gong! The Banker of Bhong! Isn't your generous young heart stirred to any extent by the prospect? I am given to understand – '

'I've a jolly good mind to chuck up the whole thing and become a pro. I've got a birth qualification for Surrey. It's about the only thing I could do any good at.'

Psmith's manner became fatherly.

'*You're* all right,' he said. 'The hot weather has given you that tired feeling. What you want is a change of air. We will pop down together hand in hand this week-end to some seaside resort. You shall build sand castles, while I lie on the beach and read the paper. In the evening we will listen to the band, or stroll on the esplanade, not so much because we want to, as to give the natives a treat. Possibly, if the weather continues warm, we may even paddle. A vastly exhilarating pastime, I am led to believe, and *so* strengthening for the ankles. And on Monday morning we will return, bronzed and bursting with health, to our toil once more.'

'I'm going to bed,' said Mike, rising.

Psmith watched him lounge from the room, and shook his head sadly. All was not well with his confidential secretary and adviser.

The next day, which was a Thursday, found Mike no more reconciled to the prospect of spending from ten till five in the company of Mr Gregory and the ledgers. He was silent at breakfast, and Psmith, seeing that things were still wrong, abstained from conversation. Mike propped the *Sportsman* up against the hot-water jug, and read the cricket news. His county, captained by brother Joe, had, as he had learned already from yesterday's evening paper, beaten Sussex by five wickets at Brighton. Today they were due to play Middlesex at Lord's. Mike thought that he would try to get off early, and go and see some of the first day's play.

As events turned out, he got off a good deal earlier, and saw a good deal more of the first day's play than he had anticipated.

He had just finished the preliminary stages of the morning's work, which consisted mostly of washing his hands, changing his coat, and eating a section of a pen-holder, when William, the messenger, approached.

'You're wanted on the 'phone, Mr Jackson.'

The New Asiatic Bank, unlike the majority of London banks, was on the telephone, a fact which Psmith found a great convenience when securing seats at the theatre. Mike went to the box and took up the receiver.

'Hullo!' he said.

'Who's that?' said an agitated voice. 'Is that you, Mike? I'm Joe.'

'Hullo, Joe,' said Mike. 'What's up? I'm coming to see you this evening. I'm going to try and get off early.'

'Look here, Mike, are you busy at the bank just now?'

'Not at the moment. There's never anything much going on before eleven.'

'I mean, are you busy today? Could you possibly manage to get off and play for us against Middlesex?'

Mike nearly dropped the receiver.

'What?' he cried.

'There's been the dickens of a mix-up. We're one short, and you're our only hope. We can't possibly get another man in the time. We start in half an hour. Can you play?'

For the space of, perhaps, one minute, Mike thought.

'Well?' said Joe's voice.

The sudden vision of Lord's ground, all green and cool in the morning sunlight, was too much for Mike's resolution, sapped as it was by days of restlessness. The feeling surged over him that whatever happened afterwards, the joy of the match in perfect weather on a perfect wicket would make it worth while. What did it matter what happened afterwards?

'All right, Joe,' he said. 'I'll hop into a cab now, and go and get my things.'

'Good man,' said Joe, hugely relieved.

26. Breaking the News

Dashing away from the call-box, Mike nearly cannoned into Psmith, who was making his way pensively to the telephone with the object of ringing up the box office of the Haymarket Theatre.

'Sorry,' said Mike. 'Hullo, Smith.'

'Hullo indeed,' said Psmith, courteously. 'I rejoice, Comrade Jackson, to find you going about your commercial duties like a young bomb. How is it, people repeatedly ask me, that Comrade Jackson contrives to catch his employer's eye and win the friendly smile from the head of his department? My reply is that where others walk, Comrade Jackson runs. Where others stroll, Comrade Jackson legs it like a highly-trained mustang of the prairie. He does not loiter. He gets back to his department bathed in perspiration, in level time. He – '

'I say, Smith,' said Mike, 'you might do me a favour.'

'A thousand. Say on.'

'Just look in at the Fixed Deposits and tell old Gregory that I shan't be with him today, will you? I haven't time myself. I must rush!'

Psmith screwed his eyeglass into his eye, and examined Mike carefully.

'What exactly – ?' be began.

'Tell the old ass I've popped off.'

'Just so, just so,' murmured Psmith, as one who assents to a thoroughly reasonable proposition. 'Tell him you have popped off. It shall be done. But it is within the bounds of possibility that Comrade Gregory may inquire further. Could you give me some inkling as to why you are popping?'

'My brother Joe has just rung me up from Lords. The county are playing Middlesex and they're one short. He wants me to roll up.'

Psmith shook his head sadly.

'I don't wish to interfere in any way,' he said, 'but I suppose you realize that, by acting thus, you are to some extent knocking the stuffing out of your chances of becoming manager of this bank? If you dash off now, I shouldn't count too much on that marrying the Governor's daughter scheme I sketched out for you last night. I doubt whether this is going to help you to hold the gorgeous East in fee, and all that sort of thing.'

'Oh, dash the gorgeous East.'

'By all means,' said Psmith obligingly. 'I just thought I'd mention it. I'll look in at Lord's this afternoon. I shall send my card up to you, and trust to your sympathetic cooperation to enable me to effect an entry into the pavilion on my face. My father is coming up to London today. I'll bring him along, too.'

'Right ho. Dash it, it's twenty to. So long. See you at Lord's.'

Psmith looked after his retreating form till it had vanished through the swing-door, and shrugged his shoulders resignedly, as if disclaiming all responsibility.

'He has gone without his hat,' he murmured. 'It seems to me that this is practically a case of running amok. And now to break the news to bereaved Comrade Gregory.'

He abandoned his intention of ringing up the Haymarket Theatre, and turning away from the call-box, walked meditatively down the aisle till he came to the Fixed Deposits Department, where the top of Mr Gregory's head was to be seen over the glass barrier, as he applied himself to his work.

Psmith, resting his elbows on the top of the barrier and holding his head between his hands, eyed the absorbed toiler for a moment in silence, then emitted a hollow groan.

Mr Gregory, who was ruling a line in a ledger – most of the work in the Fixed Deposits Department consisted of ruling lines in ledgers, sometimes in black ink, sometimes in red – started as if he had been stung, and made a complete mess of the ruled line. He lifted a fiery, bearded face, and met Psmith's eye, which shone with kindly sympathy.

He found words.

'What the dickens are you standing there for, mooing like a blanked cow?' he inquired.

'I was groaning,' explained Psmith with quiet dignity. 'And why was I groaning?' he continued. 'Because a shadow has fallen on the Fixed Deposits Department. Comrade Jackson, the Pride of the Office, has gone.'

Mr Gregory rose from his seat.

'I don't know who the dickens you are – ' he began.

'I am Psmith,' said the old Etonian.

'Oh, you're Smith, are you?'

'With a preliminary P. Which, however, is not sounded.'

'And what's all this dashed nonsense about Jackson?'

'He is gone. Gone like the dew from the petal of a rose.'

'Gone! Where's he gone to?'

'Lord's.'

'What lord's?'

Psmith waved his hand gently.

'You misunderstand me. Comrade Jackson has not gone to mix with any member of our gay and thoughtless aristocracy. He has gone to Lord's cricket ground.'

Mr Gregory's beard bristled even more than was its wont.

'What!' he roared. 'Gone to watch a cricket match! Gone – !'

'Not to watch. To play. An urgent summons I need not say. Nothing but an urgent summons could have wrenched him from your very delightful society, I am sure.'

Mr Gregory glared.

'I don't want any of your impudence,' he said.

Psmith nodded gravely.

'We all have these curious likes and dislikes,' he said tolerantly. 'You do not like my impudence. Well, well, some people don't. And now, having broken the sad news, I will return to my own department.'

'Half a minute. You come with me and tell this yarn of yours to Mr Bickersdyke.'

'You think it would interest, amuse him? Perhaps you are right. Let us buttonhole Comrade Bickersdyke.'

Mr Bickersdyke was disengaged. The head of the Fixed Deposits Department stumped into the room. Psmith followed at a more leisurely pace.

'Allow me,' he said with a winning smile, as Mr Gregory opened his mouth to speak, 'to take this opportunity of congratulating you on your success at the election. A narrow but well-deserved victory.'

There was nothing cordial in the manager's manner.

'What do you want?' he said.

'Myself, nothing,' said Psmith. 'But I understand that Mr Gregory has some communication to make.'

'Tell Mr Bickersdyke that story of yours,' said Mr Gregory.

'Surely,' said Psmith reprovingly, 'this is no time for anecdotes. Mr Bickersdyke is busy. He –'

'Tell him what you told me about Jackson.'

Mr Bickersdyke looked up inquiringly.

'Jackson,' said Psmith, 'has been obliged to absent himself from work today owing to an urgent summons from his brother, who, I understand, has suffered a bereavement.'

'It's a lie,' roared Mr Gregory. 'You told me yourself he'd gone to play in a cricket match.'

'True. As I said, he received an urgent summons from his brother.'

'What about the bereavement, then?'

'The team was one short. His brother was very distressed about it. What could Comrade Jackson do? Could he refuse to help his brother when it was in his power? His generous nature is a byword. He did the only possible thing. He consented to play.'

Mr Bickersdyke spoke.

'Am I to understand,' he asked, with sinister calm, 'that Mr Jackson has left his work and gone off to play in a cricket match?'

'Something of that sort has, I believe, happened,' said Psmith. 'He knew, of course,' he added, bowing gracefully in Mr Gregory's direction, 'that he was leaving his work in thoroughly competent hands.'

'Thank you,' said Mr Bickersdyke. 'That will do. You will help Mr Gregory in his department for the time being, Mr Smith. I will arrange for somebody to take your place in your own department.'

'It will be a pleasure,' murmured Psmith.

'Show Mr Smith what he has to do, Mr Gregory,' said the manager.

They left the room.

'How curious, Comrade Gregory,' mused Psmith, as they went, 'are the workings of Fate! A moment back, and your life was a blank. Comrade Jackson, that prince of Fixed Depositors, had gone. How, you said to yourself despairingly, can his place be filled? Then the cloud broke, and the sun shone out again. *I* came to help you. What you lose on the swings, you make up on the roundabouts. Now show me what I have to do, and then let us make this department sizzle. You have drawn a good ticket, Comrade Gregory.'

27. At Lord's

Mike got to Lord's just as the umpires moved out into the field. He raced round to the pavilion. Joe met him on the stairs.

'It's all right,' he said. 'No hurry. We've won the toss. I've put you in fourth wicket.'

'Right ho,' said Mike. 'Glad we haven't to field just yet.'

'We oughtn't to have to field today if we don't chuck our wickets away.'

'Good wicket?'

'Like a billiard-table. I'm glad you were able to come. Have any difficulty in getting away?'

Joe Jackson's knowledge of the workings of a bank was of the slightest. He himself had never, since he left Oxford, been in a position where there were obstacles to getting off to play in first-class cricket. By profession he was agent to a sporting baronet whose hobby was the cricket of the county, and so, far from finding any difficulty in playing for the county, he was given to understand by his employer that that was his chief duty. It never occurred to him that Mike might find his bank less amenable in the matter of giving leave. His only fear, when he rang Mike up that morning, had been that this might be a particularly busy day at the New Asiatic Bank. If there was no special rush of work, he took it for granted that Mike would simply go to the manager, ask for leave to play in the match, and be given it with a beaming smile.

Mike did not answer the question, but asked one on his own account.

'How did you happen to be short?' he said.

'It was rotten luck. It was like this. We were altering our team after the Sussex match, to bring in Ballard, Keene, and Willis. They couldn't get down to Brighton, as the 'Varsity had a match, but there was nothing on for them in the last half of the week, so they'd promised to roll up.'

Ballard, Keene, and Willis were members of the Cambridge

team, all very capable performers and much in demand by the county, when they could get away to play for it.

'Well?' said Mike.

'Well, we all came up by train from Brighton last night. But these three asses had arranged to motor down from Cambridge early today, and get here in time for the start. What happens? Why, Willis, who fancies himself as a chauffeur, undertakes to do the driving; and naturally, being an absolute rotter, goes and smashes up the whole concern just outside St Albans. The first thing I knew of it was when I got to Lord's at half past ten, and found a wire waiting for me to say that they were all three of them crocked, and couldn't possibly play. I tell you, it was a bit of a jar to get half an hour before the match started. Willis has sprained his ankle, apparently; Keene's damaged his wrist; and Ballard has smashed his collar-bone. I don't suppose they'll be able to play in the 'Varsity match. Rotten luck for Cambridge. Well, fortunately we'd had two reserve pros. with us at Brighton, who had come up to London with the team in case they might be wanted, so, with them, we were only one short. Then I thought of you. That's how it was.'

'I see,' said Mike. 'Who are the pros?'

'Davis and Brockley. Both bowlers. It weakens our batting a lot. Ballard or Willis might have got a stack of runs on this wicket. Still, we've got a certain amount of batting as it is. We oughtn't to do badly, if we're careful. You've been getting some practice, I suppose, this season?'

'In a sort of a way. Nets and so on. No matches of any importance.'

'Dash it, I wish you'd had a game or two in decent class cricket. Still, nets are better than nothing, I hope you'll be in form. We may want a pretty long knock from you, if things go wrong. These men seem to be settling down all right, thank goodness,' he added, looking out of the window at the county's first pair, Warrington and Mills, two professionals, who, as the result of ten minutes' play, had put up twenty.

'I'd better go and change,' said Mike, picking up his bag. 'You're in first wicket, I suppose?'

'Yes. And Reggie, second wicket.'

Reggie was another of Mike's brothers, not nearly so fine a player as Joe, but a sound bat, who generally made runs if allowed to stay in.

Mike changed, and went out into the little balcony at the top of the pavilion. He had it to himself. There were not many spectators in the pavilion at this early stage of the game.

There are few more restful places, if one wishes to think, than the upper balconies of Lord's pavilion. Mike, watching the game making its leisurely progress on the turf below, set himself seriously to review the situation in all its aspects. The exhilaration of bursting the bonds had begun to fade, and he found himself able to look into the matter of his desertion and weigh up the consequences. There was no doubt that he had cut the painter once and for all. Even a friendly-disposed management could hardly overlook what he had done. And the management of the New Asiatic Bank was the very reverse of friendly. Mr Bickersdyke, he knew, would jump at this chance of getting rid of him. He realized that he must look on his career in the bank as a closed book. It was definitely over, and he must now think about the future.

It was not a time for half-measures. He could not go home. He must carry the thing through, now that he had begun, and find something definite to do, to support himself.

There seemed only one opening for him. What could he do, he asked himself. Just one thing. He could play cricket. It was by his cricket that he must live. He would have to become a professional. Could he get taken on? That was the question. It was impossible that he should play for his own county on his residential qualification. He could not appear as a professional in the same team in which his brothers were playing as amateurs. He must stake all on his birth qualification for Surrey.

On the other hand, had he the credentials which Surrey would want? He had a school reputation. But was that enough? He could not help feeling that it might not be.

Thinking it over more tensely than he had ever thought over anything in his whole life, he saw clearly that everything depended on what sort of show he made in this match which was now in progress. It was his big chance. If he succeeded, all would be well. He did not care to think what his position would be if he did not succeed.

A distant appeal and a sound of clapping from the crowd broke in on his thoughts. Mills was out, caught at the wicket. The telegraph-board gave the total as forty-eight. Not sensational. The success of the team depended largely on what sort of a start the two professionals made.

The clapping broke out again as Joe made his way down the steps. Joe, as an All England player, was a favourite with the crowd.

Mike watched him play an over in his strong, graceful style: then it suddenly occurred to him that he would like to know how matters had gone at the bank in his absence.

He went down to the telephone, rang up the bank, and asked for Psmith.

Presently the familiar voice made itself heard.

'Hullo, Smith.'

'Hullo. Is that Comrade Jackson? How are things progressing?'

'Fairly well. We're in first. We've lost one wicket, and the fifty's just up. I say, what's happened at the bank?'

'I broke the news to Comrade Gregory. A charming personality. I feel that we shall be friends.'

'Was he sick?'

'In a measure, yes. Indeed, I may say he practically foamed at the mouth. I explained the situation, but he was not to be appeased. He jerked me into the presence of Comrade Bickersdyke, with whom I had a brief but entertaining chat. He had not a great deal to say, but he listened attentively to my narrative, and eventually told me off to take your place in the Fixed Deposits. That melancholy task I am now performing to the best of my ability. I find the work a little trying. There is too much ledger-lugging to be done for my simple tastes. I have been hauling ledgers from the safe all the morning. The cry is beginning to go round, "Psmith is willing, but can his physique stand the strain?" In the excitement of the moment just now I dropped a somewhat massive tome on to Comrade Gregory's foot, unfortunately, I understand, the foot in which he has of late been suffering twinges of gout. I passed the thing off with ready tact, but I cannot deny that there was a certain temporary coolness, which, indeed, is not yet past. These things, Comrade Jackson, are the whirlpools in the quiet stream of commercial life.'

'Have I got the sack.'

'No official pronouncement has been made to me as yet on the subject, but I think I should advise you, if you are offered another job in the course of the day, to accept it. I cannot say that you are precisely the pet of the management just at present. However, I have ideas for your future, which I will divulge when we meet. I propose to slide coyly from the office at about four o'clock. I am meeting my father at that hour. We shall come straight on to Lord's.'

'Right ho,' said Mike. 'I'll be looking out for you.'

'Is there any little message I can give Comrade Gregory from you?'

'You can give him my love, if you like.'

'It shall be done. Good-bye.'

'Good-bye.'

Mike replaced the receiver, and went up to his balcony again.

As soon as his eye fell on the telegraph-board he saw with a start that things had been moving rapidly in his brief absence. The numbers of the batsmen on the board were three and five.

'Great Scott!' he cried. 'Why, I'm in next. What on earth's been happening?'

He put on his pads hurriedly, expecting every moment that a wicket would fall and find him unprepared. But the batsmen were still together when he rose, ready for the fray, and went downstairs to get news.

He found his brother Reggie in the dressing-room.

'What's happened?' he said. 'How were you out?'

'L.b.w.,' said Reggie. 'Goodness knows how it happened. My eyesight must be going. I mistimed the thing altogether.'

'How was Warrington out?'

'Caught in the slips.'

'By Jove!' said Mike. 'This is pretty rocky. Three for sixty-one. We shall get mopped.'

'Unless you and Joe do something. There's no earthly need to get out. The wicket's as good as you want, and the bowling's nothing special. Well played, Joe!'

A beautiful glide to leg by the greatest of the Jacksons had rolled up against the pavilion rails. The fieldsmen changed across for the next over.

'If only Peters stops a bit –' began Mike, and broke off. Peters' off stump was lying at an angle of forty-five degrees.

'Well, he hasn't,' said Reggie grimly. 'Silly ass, why did he hit at that one? All he'd got to do was to stay in with Joe. Now it's up to you. Do try and do something, or we'll be out under the hundred.'

Mike waited till the outcoming batsman had turned in at the professionals' gate. Then he walked down the steps and out into the open, feeling more nervous than he had felt since that far-off day when he had first gone in to bat for Wrykyn against the M.C.C. He found his thoughts flying back to that occasion. Today, as then, everything seemed very distant and unreal. The spectators were miles away. He had often been to Lord's as a spectator, but the place seemed entirely unfamiliar now. He felt as if he were in a strange land.

He was conscious of Joe leaving the crease to meet him on his way. He smiled feebly. 'Buck up,' said Joe in that robust way of his which was so heartening. 'Nothing in the bowling, and the wicket like a shirt-front. Play just as if you were at the nets. And for goodness' sake don't try to score all your runs in the first over. Stick in, and we've got them.'

Mike smiled again more feebly than before, and made a weird gurgling noise in his throat.

It had been the Middlesex fast bowler who had destroyed Peters. Mike was not sorry. He did not object to fast bowling. He took guard, and looked round him, taking careful note of the positions of the slips.

As usual, once he was at the wicket the paralysed feeling left him. He became conscious again of his power. Dash it all, what was there to be afraid of? He was a jolly good bat, and he would jolly well show them that he was, too.

The fast bowler, with a preliminary bound, began his run. Mike settled himself into position, his whole soul concentrated on the ball. Everything else was wiped from his mind.

28. Psmith Arranges his Future

It was exactly four o'clock when Psmith, sliding unostentatiously from his stool, flicked divers pieces of dust from the leg of his trousers, and sidled towards the basement, where he was wont to keep his hat during business hours. He was aware that it would be a matter of some delicacy to leave the bank at that hour. There was a certain quantity of work still to be done in the Fixed Deposits Department – work in which, by rights, as Mike's understudy, he should have lent a sympathetic and helping hand. 'But what of that?' he mused, thoughtfully smoothing his hat with his knuckles. 'Comrade Gregory is a man who takes such an enthusiastic pleasure in his duties that he will go singing about the office when he discovers that he has got a double lot of work to do.'

With this comforting thought, he started on his perilous journey to the open air. As he walked delicately, not courting observation, he reminded himself of the hero of 'Pilgrim's Progress'. On all sides of him lay fearsome beasts, lying in wait to pounce upon him. At any moment Mr Gregory's hoarse roar might shatter the comparative stillness, or the sinister note of Mr Bickersdyke make itself heard.

'However,' said Psmith philosophically, 'these are Life's Trials, and must be borne patiently.'

A roundabout route, *via* the Postage and Inwards Bills Departments, took him to the swing-doors. It was here that the danger became acute. The doors were well within view of the Fixed Deposits Department, and Mr Gregory had an eye compared with which that of an eagle was more or less bleared.

Psmith looked up. Mr Gregory was leaning over the barrier manner. As he did so a bellow rang through the office, causing a timid customer, who had come in to arrange about an overdraft, to lose his nerve completely and postpone his business till the following afternoon.

Psmith looked up. Mr Gregory was leaning over the barrier

which divided his lair from the outer world, and gesticulating violently.

'Where are you going,' roared the head of the Fixed Deposits.

Psmith did not reply. With a benevolent smile and a gesture intended to signify all would come right in the future, he slid through the swing-doors, and began to move down the street at a somewhat swifter pace than was his habit.

Once round the corner he slackened his speed.

'This can't go on,' he said to himself. 'This life of commerce is too great a strain. One is practically a hunted hare. Either the heads of my department must refrain from View Halloos when they observe me going for a stroll, or I abandon Commerce for some less exacting walk in life.'

He removed his hat, and allowed the cool breeze to play upon his forehead. The episode had been disturbing.

He was to meet his father at the Mansion House. As he reached that land-mark he saw with approval that punctuality was a virtue of which he had not the sole monopoly in the Smith family. His father was waiting for him at the tryst.

'Certainly, my boy,' said Mr Smith senior, all activity in a moment, when Psmith had suggested going to Lord's. 'Excellent. We must be getting on. We must not miss a moment of the match. Bless my soul: I haven't seen a first-class match this season. Where's a cab? Hi, cabby! No, that one's got some one in it. There's another. Hi! Here, lunatic! Are you blind? Good, he's seen us. That's right. Here he comes. Lord's Cricket Ground, cabby, as quick as you can. Jump in, Rupert, my boy, jump in.'

Psmith rarely jumped. He entered the cab with something of the stateliness of an old Roman Emperor boarding his chariot, and settled himself comfortably in his seat. Mr Smith dived in like a rabbit.

A vendor of newspapers came to the cab thrusting an evening paper into the interior. Psmith bought it.

'Let's see how they're getting on,' he said, opening the paper. 'Where are we? Lunch scores. Lord's. Aha! Comrade Jackson is in form.'

'Jackson?' said Mr Smith. 'is that the same youngster you brought home last summer? The batsman? Is he playing today?'

'He was not out thirty at lunch-time. He would appear to be making something of a stand with his brother Joe, who has made sixty-one up to the moment of going to press. It's possible he may still be in when we get there. In which case we shall not be able to slide into the pavilion.'

'A grand bat, that boy. I said so last summer. Better than any of his brothers. He's in the bank with you, isn't he?'

'He was this morning. I doubt, however, whether he can be said to be still in that position.'

'Eh? what? How's that?'

'There was some slight friction between him and the management. They wished him to be glued to his stool; he preferred to play for the county. I think we may say that Comrade Jackson has secured the Order of the Boot.'

'What? Do you mean to say – ?'

Psmith related briefly the history of Mike's departure.

Mr Smith listened with interest.

'Well,' he said at last, 'hang me if I blame the boy. It's a sin cooping up a fellow who can bat like that in a bank. I should have done the same myself in his place.'

Psmith smoothed his waistcoat.

'Do you know, father,' he said, 'this bank business is far from being much of a catch. Indeed, I should describe it definitely as a bit off. I have given it a fair trial, and I now denounce it unhesitatingly as a shade too thick.'

'What? Are you getting tired of it?'

'Not precisely tired. But, after considerable reflection, I have come to the conclusion that my talents lie elsewhere. At lugging ledgers I am among the also-rans – a mere cipher. I have been wanting to speak to you about this for some time. If you have no objection, I should like to go to the Bar.'

'The Bar? Well – '

'I fancy I should make a pretty considerable hit as a barrister.'

Mr Smith reflected. The idea had not occurred to him before. Now that it was suggested, his always easily-fired imagination took hold of it readily. There was a good deal to be said for the Bar as a career. Psmith knew his father, and he knew that the thing was practically as good as settled. It was a new idea, and as such was bound to be favourably received.

'What I should do, if I were you,' he went on, as if he were advising a friend on some course of action certain to bring him profit and pleasure, 'is to take me away from the bank at once. Don't wait. There is no time like the present. Let me hand in my resignation tomorrow. The blow to the management, especially to Comrade Bickersdyke, will be a painful one, but it is the truest kindness to administer it swiftly. Let me resign tomorrow, and devote my time to quiet study. Then I can pop up to Cambridge next term, and all will be well.'

'I'll think it over – ' began Mr Smith.

'Let us hustle,' urged Psmith. 'Let us Do It Now. It is the only way. Have I your leave to shoot in my resignation to Comrade Bickersdyke tomorrow morning?'

Mr Smith hesitated for a moment, then made up his mind.

'Very well,' he said. 'I really think it is a good idea. There are great opportunities open to a barrister. I wish we had thought of it before.'

'I am not altogether sorry that we did not,' said Psmith. 'I have enjoyed the chances my commercial life has given me of associating with such a man as Comrade Bickersdyke. In many ways a master-mind. But perhaps it is as well to close the chapter. How it happened it is hard to say, but somehow I fancy I did not precisely hit it off with Comrade Bickersdyke. With Psmith, the worker, he had no fault to find; but it seemed to me sometimes, during our festive evenings together at the club, that all was not well. From little, almost imperceptible signs I have suspected now and then that he would just as soon have been without my company. One cannot explain these things. It must have been some incompatibility of temperament. Perhaps he will manage to bear up at my departure. But here we are,' he added, as the cab drew up. 'I wonder if Comrade Jackson is still going strong.'

They passed through the turnstile, and caught sight of the telegraph-board.

'By Jove!' said Psmith, 'he is. I don't know if he's number three or number six. I expect he's number six. In which case he has got ninety-eight. We're just in time to see his century.'

29. And Mike's

For nearly two hours Mike had been experiencing the keenest pleasure that it had ever fallen to his lot to feel. From the moment he took his first ball till the luncheon interval he had suffered the acutest discomfort. His nervousness had left him to a great extent, but he had never really settled down. Sometimes by luck, and sometimes by skill, he had kept the ball out of his wicket; but he was scratching, and he knew it. Not for a single over had he been comfortable. On several occasions he had edged balls to leg and through the slips in quite an inferior manner, and it was seldom that he managed to hit with the centre of the bat.

Nobody is more alive to the fact that he is not playing up to his true form than the batsman. Even though his score mounted little by little into the twenties, Mike was miserable. If this was the best he could do on a perfect wicket, he felt there was not much hope for him as a professional.

The poorness of his play was accentuated by the brilliance of Joe's. Joe combined science and vigour to a remarkable degree. He laid on the wood with a graceful robustness which drew much cheering from the crowd. Beside him Mike was oppressed by that leaden sense of moral inferiority which weighs on a man who has turned up to dinner in ordinary clothes when everybody else has dressed. He felt awkward and conspicuously out of place.

Then came lunch – and after lunch a glorious change.

Volumes might be written on the cricket lunch and the influence it has on the run of the game; how it undoes one man, and sends another back to the fray like a giant refreshed; how it turns the brilliant fast bowler into the sluggish medium, and the nervous bat into the masterful smiter.

On Mike its effect was magical. He lunched wisely and well, chewing his food with the concentration of a thirty-three-bites a mouthful crank, and drinking dry ginger-ale. As he walked out with Joe after the interval he knew that a change had taken place in him. His nerve had come back, and with it his form.

It sometimes happens at cricket that when one feels particularly fit one gets snapped in the slips in the first over, or clean bowled by a full toss; but neither of these things happened to Mike. He stayed in, and began to score. Now there were no edgings through the slips and snicks to leg. He was meeting the ball in the centre of the bat, and meeting it vigorously. Two boundaries in successive balls off the fast bowler, hard, clean drives past extra-cover, put him at peace with all the world. He was on top. He had found himself.

Joe, at the other end, resumed his brilliant career. His century and Mike's fifty arrived in the same over. The bowling began to grow loose.

Joe, having reached his century, slowed down somewhat, and Mike took up the running. The score rose rapidly.

A leg-theory bowler kept down the pace of the run-getting for a time, but the bowlers at the other end continued to give away runs. Mike's score passed from sixty to seventy, from seventy to eighty, from eighty to ninety. When the Smiths, father and son, came on to the ground the total was ninety-eight. Joe had made a hundred and thirty-three.

Mike reached his century just as Psmith and his father took their seats. A square cut off the slow bowler was just too wide for point to get to. By the time third man had sprinted across and returned the ball the batsmen had run two.

Mr Smith was enthusiastic.

'I tell you,' he said to Psmith, who was clapping in a gently encouraging manner, 'the boy's a wonderful bat. I said so when he was down with us. I remember telling him so myself. "I've seen your brothers play," I said, "and you're better than any of them." I remember it distinctly. He'll be playing for England in another year or two. Fancy putting a cricketer like that into the City! It's a crime.'

'I gather,' said Psmith, 'that the family coffers had got a bit low. It was necessary for Comrade Jackson to do something by way of saving the Old Home.'

'He ought to be at the University. Look, he's got that man away to the boundary again. They'll never get him out.'

At six o'clock the partnership was broken, Joe running himself out in trying to snatch a single where no single was. He had made a hundred and eighty-nine.

Mike flung himself down on the turf with mixed feelings. He was sorry Joe was out, but he was very glad indeed of the chance of a rest. He was utterly fagged. A half-day match once a week is no training for first-class cricket. Joe, who had been playing all the season, was as tough as india-rubber, and trotted into the pavilion as fresh as if he had been having a brief spell at the nets. Mike, on the other hand, felt that he simply wanted to be dropped into a cold bath and left there indefinitely. There was only another half-hour's play, but he doubted if he could get through it.

He dragged himself up wearily as Joe's successor arrived at the wickets. He had crossed Joe before the latter's downfall, and it was his turn to take the bowling.

Something seemed to have gone out of him. He could not time the ball properly. The last ball of the over looked like a half-volley, and he hit out at it. But it was just short of a half-volley, and his stroke arrived too soon. The bowler, running in the direction of mid-on, brought off an easy c.-and-b.

Mike turned away towards the pavilion. He heard the gradually swelling applause in a sort of dream. It seemed to him hours before he reached the dressing-room.

He was sitting on a chair, wishing that somebody would come along and take off his pads, when Psmith's card was brought to him. A few moments later the old Etonian appeared in person.

'Hullo, Smith,' said Mike, 'By Jove! I'm done.'

' "How Little Willie Saved the Match," ' said Psmith. 'What you want is one of those gin and ginger-beers we hear so much about. Remove those pads, and let us flit downstairs in search of a couple. Well, Comrade Jackson, you have fought the good fight this day. My father sends his compliments. He is dining out, or he would have come up. He is going to look in at the flat latish.'

'How many did I get?' asked Mike. 'I was so jolly done I didn't think of looking.'

'A hundred and forty-eight of the best,' said Psmith. 'What will they say at the old homestead about this? Are you ready? Then let us test this fruity old ginger-beer of theirs.'

The two batsmen who had followed the big stand were apparently having a little stand all of their own. No more wickets fell before the drawing of stumps. Psmith waited for Mike while he changed, and carried him off in a cab to Simpson's, a restaurant which, as he justly observed, offered two great advantages, namely, that you need not dress, and, secondly, that you paid your half-crown, and were then at liberty to eat till you were helpless, if you felt so disposed, without extra charge.

Mike stopped short of this giddy height of mastication, but consumed enough to make him feel a great deal better. Psmith eyed his inroads on the menu with approval.

'There is nothing,' he said, 'like victualling up before an ordeal.'

'What's the ordeal?' said Mike.

'I propose to take you round to the club anon, where I trust we shall find Comrade Bickersdyke. We have much to say to one another.'

'Look here, I'm hanged – ' began Mike.

'Yes, you must be there,' said Psmith. 'Your presence will serve to cheer Comrade B. up. Fate compels me to deal him a nasty blow, and he will want sympathy. I have got to break it to him that I am leaving the bank.'

'What, are you going to chuck it?'

Psmith inclined his head.

'The time,' he said, 'has come to part. It has served its turn. The startled whisper runs round the City. "Psmith has had sufficient." '

'What are you going to do?'

'I propose to enter the University of Cambridge, and there to study the intricacies of the Law, with a view to having a subsequent dash at becoming Lord Chancellor.'

'By Jove!' said Mike, 'you're lucky. I wish I were coming too.'

Psmith knocked the ash off his cigarette.

'Are you absolutely set on becoming a pro?' he asked.

'It depends on what you call set. It seems to me it's about all I can do.'

'I can offer you a not entirely scaly job,' said Smith, 'if you feel like taking it. In the course of conversation with my father during the match this afternoon, I gleaned the fact that he is anxious to secure your services as a species of agent. The vast Psmith estates, it seems, need a bright boy to keep an eye upon them. Are you prepared to accept the post?'

Mike stared.

'Me! Dash it all, how old do you think I am? I'm only nineteen.'

'I had suspected as much from the alabaster clearness of your unwrinkled brow. But my father does not wish you to enter upon your duties immediately. There would be a preliminary interval of three, possibly four, years at Cambridge, during which I presume, you would be learning divers facts concerning spuds, turmuts, and the like. At least,' said Psmith airily, 'I suppose so. Far be it from me to dictate the line of your researches.'

'Then I'm afraid it's off,' said Mike gloomily. 'My pater couldn't afford to send me to Cambridge.'

'That obstacle,' said Psmith, 'can be surmounted. You would, of course, accompany me to Cambridge, in the capacity, which you enjoy at the present moment, of my confidential secretary and adviser. Any expenses that might crop up would be defrayed from the Psmith family chest.'

Mike's eyes opened wide again.

'Do you mean,' he asked bluntly, 'that your pater would pay for me at the 'Varsity? No I say – dash it – I mean, I couldn't – '

'Do you suggest,' said Psmith, raising his eyebrows, 'that I should go to the University *without* a confidential secretary and adviser?'

'No, but I mean – ' protested Mike.

'Then that's settled,' said Psmith. 'I knew you would not desert me in my hour of need, Comrade Jackson. "What will you do," asked my father, alarmed for my safety, "among these wild undergraduates? I fear for my Rupert." "Have no fear, father," I replied. "Comrade Jackson will be beside me." His face brightened immediately. "Comrade Jackson," he said, "is a man in whom I have the supremest confidence. If he is with you I shall sleep easy of nights." It was after that that the conversation drifted to the subject of agents.'

Psmith called for the bill and paid it in the affable manner of a monarch signing a charter. Mike sat silent, his mind in a whirl. He saw exactly what had happened. He could almost hear Psmith talking his father into agreeing with his scheme. He

could think of nothing to say. As usually happened in any
emotional crisis in his life, words absolutely deserted him. The
thing was too big. Anything he could say would sound too
feeble. When a friend has solved all your difficulties and
smoothed out all the rough places which were looming in your
path, you cannot thank him as if he had asked you to lunch. The
occasion demanded some neat, polished speech; and neat, polished speeches were beyond Mike.

'I say, Psmith – ' he began.

Psmith rose.

'Let us now,' he said, 'collect our hats and meander to the
club, where, I have no doubt, we shall find Comrade Bickersdyke, all unconscious of impending misfortune, dreaming
pleasantly over coffee and a cigar in the lower smoking-
room.'

30. The Last Sad Farewells

As it happened, that was precisely what Mr Bickersdyke was
doing. He was feeling thoroughly pleased with life. For nearly
nine months Psmith had been to him a sort of spectre at the
feast inspiring him with an ever-present feeling of discomfort
which he had found impossible to shake off. And tonight he saw
his way of getting rid of him.

At five minutes past four Mr Gregory, crimson and wrathful,
had plunged into his room with a long statement of how
Psmith, deputed to help in the life and thought of the Fixed
Deposits Department, had left the building at four o'clock,
when there was still another hour and a half's work to be
done.

Moreover, Mr Gregory deposed, the errant one, seen sliding
out of the swinging door, and summoned in a loud, clear voice
to come back, had flatly disobeyed and had gone upon his way.
'Grinning at me,' said the aggrieved Mr Gregory, 'like a dashed
ape.' A most unjust description of the sad, sweet smile which
Psmith had bestowed upon him from the doorway.

Ever since that moment Mr Bickersdyke had felt that there
was a silver lining to the cloud. Hitherto Psmith had left
nothing to be desired in the manner in which he performed his
work. His righteousness in the office had clothed him as in a suit
of mail. But now he had slipped. To go off an hour and a half
before the proper time, and to refuse to return when summoned
by the head of his department – these were offences for which
he could be dismissed without fuss. Mr Bickersdyke looked
forward to tomorrow's interview with his employee.

Meanwhile, having enjoyed an excellent dinner, he was now,
as Psmith had predicted, engaged with a cigar and a cup of
coffee in the lower smoking-room of the Senior Conservative
Club.

Psmith and Mike entered the room when he was about half
through these luxuries.

Psmith's first action was to summon a waiter, and order a glass of neat brandy.

'Not for myself,' he explained to Mike. 'For Comrade Bickersdyke. He is about to sustain a nasty shock, and may need a restorative at a moment's notice. For all we know, his heart may not be strong. In any case, it is safest to have a pick-me-up handy.'

He paid the waiter, and advanced across the room, followed by Mike. In his hand, extended at arm's length, he bore the glass of brandy.

Mr Bickersdyke caught sight of the procession, and started. Psmith set the brandy down very carefully on the table, beside the manager's coffee cup, and, dropping into a chair, regarded him pityingly through his eyeglass. Mike, who felt embarrassed, took a seat some little way behind his companion. This was Psmith's affair, and he proposed to allow him to do the talking.

Mr Bickersdyke, except for a slight deepening of the colour of his complexion, gave no sign of having seen them. He puffed away at his cigar, his eyes fixed on the ceiling.

'An unpleasant task lies before us,' began Psmith in a low, sorrowful voice, 'and it must not be shirked. Have I your ear, Mr Bickersdyke?'

Addressed thus directly, the manager allowed his gaze to wander from the ceiling. He eyed Psmith for a moment like an elderly basilisk, than looked back at the ceiling again.

'I shall speak to you tomorrow,' he said.

Psmith heaved a heavy sigh.

'You will not see us tomorrow,' he said, pushing the brandy a little nearer.

Mr Bickersdyke's eyes left the ceiling once more.

'What do you mean?' he said.

'Drink this,' urged Psmith sympathetically, holding out the glass. 'Be brave,' he went on rapidly. 'Time softens the harshest blows. Shocks stun us for the moment, but we recover. Little by little we come to ourselves again. Life, which we had thought could hold no more pleasure for us, gradually shows itself not wholly grey.'

Mr Bickersdyke seemed about to make an observation at this point, but Psmith, with a wave of the hand, hurried on.

'We find that the sun still shines, the birds still sing. Things which used to entertain us resume their attraction. Gradually we emerge from the soup, and begin – '

'If you have anything to say to me,' said the manager, 'I should be glad if you would say it, and go.'

'You prefer me not to break the bad news gently?' said Psmith. 'Perhaps you are wise. In a word, then,' – he picked up the brandy and held it out to him – 'Comrade Jackson and myself are leaving the bank.'

'I am aware of that,' said Mr Bickersdyke drily.

Psmith put down the glass.

'You have been told already?' he said. 'That accounts for your calm. The shock has expended its force on you, and can do no more. You are stunned. I am sorry, but it had to be. You will say that it is madness for us to offer our resignations, that our grip on the work of the bank made a prosperous career in Commerce certain for us. It may be so. But somehow we feel that our talents lie elsewhere. To Comrade Jackson the management of the Psmith estates seems the job on which he can get the rapid half-Nelson. For my own part, I feel that my long suit is the Bar. I am a poor, unready speaker, but I intend to acquire a knowledge of the Law which shall outweigh this defect. Before leaving you, I should like to say – I may speak for you as well as myself, Comrade Jackson – ?'

Mike uttered his first contribution to the conversation – a gurgle – and relapsed into silence again.

'I should like to say,' continued Psmith, 'how much Comrade Jackson and I have enjoyed our stay in the bank. The insight it has given us into your masterly handling of the intricate mechanism of the office has been a treat we would not have missed. But our place is elsewhere.'

He rose. Mike followed his example with alacrity. It occurred to Mr Bickersdyke, as they turned to go, that he had not yet been able to get in a word about their dismissal. They were drifting away with all the honours of war.

'Come back,' he cried.

Psmith paused and shook his head sadly.

'This is unmanly, Comrade Bickersdyke,' he said. 'I had not expected this. That you should be dazed by the shock was natural. But that you should beg us to reconsider our resolve and return to the bank is unworthy of you. Be a man. Bite the bullet. The first keen pang will pass. Time will soften the feeling of bereavement. You must be brave. Come, Comrade Jackson.'

Mike responded to the call without hesitation.

'We will now,' said Psmith, leading the way to the door, 'push back to the flat. My father will be round there soon.' He looked over his shoulder. Mr Bickersdyke appeared to be wrapped in thought.

'A painful business,' sighed Psmith. 'The man seems quite broken up. It had to be, however. The bank was no place for us. An excellent career in many respects, but unsuitable for you and me. It is hard on Comrade Bickersdyke, especially as he took such trouble to get me into it, but I think we may say that we are well out of the place.'

Mike's mind roamed into the future. Cambridge first, and then an open-air life of the sort he had always dreamed of. The Problem of Life seemed to him to be solved. He looked on down the years, and he could see no troubles there of any kind whatsoever. Reason suggested that there were probably one or two knocking about somewhere, but this was no time to think of them. He examined the future, and found it good.

'I should jolly well think,' he said simply, 'that we might.'

More about Penguins and Pelicans

Penguinews, which appears every month, contains details of all the new books issued by Penguins as they are published. From time to time it is supplemented by *Penguins in Print*, which is a complete list of all titles available. (There are some five thousand of these.)

A specimen copy of *Penguinews* will be sent to you free on request. For a year's issues (including the complete lists) please send 50p if you live in the British Isles, or 75p if you live elsewhere. Just write to Dept EP, Penguin Books Ltd, Harmondsworth, Middlesex, enclosing a cheque or postal order, and your name will be added to the mailing list.

In the U.S.A.: For a complete list of books available from Penguin in the United States write to Dept CS, Penguin Books Inc., 7110 Ambassador Road, Baltimore, Maryland 21207.

In Canada: For a complete list of books available from Penguin in Canada write to Penguin Books Canada Ltd, 41 Steelcase Road West, Markham, Ontario

P. G. Wodehouse

'Mr Wodehouse's idyllic world can never stale. He will continue to release future generations from captivity that may be more irksome than our own. He has made a world for us to live in and delight in' – Evelyn Waugh in a B.B.C. broadcast.

Available in Penguins:

Carry on, Jeeves
The Code of the Woosters
Service With A Smile
Stiff Upper Lip, Jeeves
Uncle Fred in the Springtime
Jeeves in the Offing

The Mating Season
The Inimitable Jeeves
Right Ho, Jeeves
The Luck of the Bodkins
Very Good, Jeeves

Not for sale in the U.S.A.